ROTOROA

ROTOROA

Amy Head

Victoria University Press

VICTORIA UNIVERSITY PRESS
Victoria University of Wellington
PO Box 600 Wellington
vup.victoria.ac.nz

A catalogue record is available from the National Library
of New Zealand

ISBN 9781776561919

Published with the assistance of a grant from

ARTS COUNCIL OF NEW ZEALAND *TOI AOTEAROA*

Printed by Printlink, Wellington

for Ruth and Sophie

Lorna

Where you lived was important. Not Takapuna, which was Lorna's neighbourhood at the time, but the house and section itself. If theirs was white-painted timber, and boxy (they could pick their own window trim); if they had a lawn and a low wall at the front and a driveway for a car, because more and more people had them then, though not them, the Vardys, not for another year; if her dad went to work in the morning and her mum was out at the washing line from time to time; in other words, if their house was near enough to being the same as everyone else's: then they'd have to be all puffed up to think anything that went on inside their own four walls mattered, wouldn't they? It couldn't make much difference if Lorna was an only child or if they tended not to invite people around. Everything important happened in the outside world, a long way off.

Who do you think it was at the door that day but two Mormon missionaries, their bikes leaned at the gate, their suits crease-free, jackets and ties on, so polite. Could they speak to her mother, they asked? So she let them in, and would her mother be willing to stay and listen for a few moments, they wanted to know. Yes she would, but they didn't know that the reason Lorna's mum listened so willingly, propped up in her armchair, was that her back was playing up that day (she would sometimes have to lie on the floor—at least once she had eased herself up from this position and told Lorna it was time they vacuumed the carpet). As it turned out, having such well-presented young men request an interview breathed life into her mum that day, the promise of something new.

For a start, both were Americans, representatives of the wider world who waltzed in and took up positions on the couch and were friendly to them, never mind what they said. More than that, they were young. They said Jesus made them happy. Well, Lorna and her mum were pleased for them. Could they come back and speak to her father? Yes of course, far better for them to explain it to him than them, so yes, please do, and when they stood to go, suits not quite the style other men might wear but so neat, Elder Cowley addressed a question not to Lorna exactly but about her: did she play sport? She'd started at high school the year before and in the basketball team a few months earlier. Yes she does, her mum said. Did she know about men's basketball, where they bounce instead of throw, and the hoop is higher, with a backboard, and Lorna had to answer this one herself. Yes she did. Had she heard of the Harlem Globetrotters? Jumpin' Johnny Wilson? The Globetrotters yes, Jumpin' Johnny no. The missionaries left gospel tracts behind.

They parked their bikes in the same spot the next day, Saturday. This time they wanted Jesus to make the Vardys happy too. Elder Cowley sat at the very front of the settee cushion, leaning forwards, speaking to Lorna's dad. 'I'd like to ask you one thing if I may.'

Lorna guessed he was about nineteen or twenty. She'd seen Americans before, when they'd visited her school, but she'd never had a conversation with one. He had doe-like eyes and short, bristling hair. He reminded her of the young men in army posters.

'Do you have difficulties in life,' Elder Cowley asked, 'things you would like to change?'

Lorna's dad placed both hands on his knees. 'Don't we all?' Her mum glanced at him. He was short and red-cheeked, her dad, and his blond hair got wild if it grew more than an inch long. She knew that from the time he'd gone to hospital and didn't have a chance to get his hair cut before he came home. He said, 'It's a funny thing that I slog away at the brickworks and it's Mum here who's got the bad back.' Not funny at all, Lorna thought. The Elders egged him on and pointed out passages in the Bible where God had solved a wide variety of problems, from hunger and floods to moral dilemmas. They mentioned Jesus and God casually, as though they lived over in Devonport, where the Mormons held their meetings. Her parents enjoyed the Elders' nodding attention, that was obvious, or they wouldn't have sent her out of the room so they could discuss different troubles she wasn't supposed to hear. When she left them sitting there, she didn't know how long this new order would last, her mum hopeful and her dad as though he'd been washed up on a beach without leaving the lounge, or if they were her new parents, permanently.

When her dad lost his temper over something small, say she'd bruised an apple and put it back in the bowl, he would find her afterwards. He'd crouch down beside her in her usual place at the side of the house—corrugated iron and fence posts and the mossy carpet between blades of grass—and he'd just stay there for a while. He wouldn't say sorry, but Lorna knew that was what he meant. Every morning before work he swept the path and driveway with a broom, never mind that the dropped seedpods might blow over from next door or that Lorna might scatter sand across them when she got home. And he stood to attention in company, almost any company. He was standing like that the day he got back from the war, when he went to collect her from school.

She was five. One day he wasn't there then he was, a father who arrived in her life instead of being around from the start. When he greeted her at the front gates, pulled up so straight and looking so serious, she was awed to think that he was going to live in their house. She couldn't have anything to say that would interest him, but it didn't matter in the end because she was too distracted to try. He walked them the wrong way home, and she grew frightened. He might not know the way. He might be taking her somewhere different. He might be the wrong person, someone else's father who had just got back from the war. She didn't recognise him and she didn't recognise those streets. When they turned a corner to see the hedge of wild currant and hear the rushing of water under the manhole cover beside the footpath—there was the wooden cat ornament attached to Old Lady Sumpter's letterbox—she was so relieved that she asked him for the treat her mother had told her to expect, something from overseas, and was crushed when he told her: 'I had better things to worry about than buying presents.'

This turned out not to be true. There were two gifts, actually. She shouldn't ask for presents, he said (it was she who didn't know the right ways of doing things, as far as he was concerned). One was a circular piece of tin with a rim, and a picture of a ship emerging from the Stars and Stripes, with the word 'Starline' across the top. This object was in fact an ashtray, not that it made any difference to Lorna at the time. He also gave her lollies she'd never seen before. Spangles, which rattled invitingly in their box, and a Sherbet Fountain, which was bliss, fizzy and soft with a liquorice straw, easily the best. She kept the Spangles and the Sherbet Fountain in the ashtray on her dressing table where they more than made up for the scare she'd had earlier. She was sure nobody at school would be able to compete with this treasure until one girl showed her the Harrods of London tin she kept her pencils in. Lorna didn't tell the girl, but she still preferred hers, because it stirred up dreams of travel and, after the lollies had been eaten, cradled sweet ghosts.

Tea was off limits in the Word of Wisdom, so her parents began their formal investigation of the faith over water. They learned about Joseph Smith, the American Revelation and a chosen people who could spread their testimony throughout the world. Lorna looked forward to seeing the Elders in the evening, in the lounge or at the table, especially Elder Cowley. She made sure she'd changed out of her school uniform into a skirt and jersey (or 'sweater') and brushed her hair, but to gussy herself up any more than that would have been immodest. They always wore their suits, but one night they arrived in raincoats with their trousers wet. When she handed each of them a towel, doing as she was told, she noticed one of their coats was hung with the tag facing outward. It was different from the ones she was used to, not yellow but a slick, dripping green. She looked for the brand, expecting something exotic, and saw an extra label had been sewn in and written on with a marker: 'If found please return to Neil Cowley'. It took her a moment to realise that this was Elder Cowley's coat. His first name was Neil. Underneath that, an address had been crossed out and replaced with another: 4 Taunton Street, Belmont. She didn't know Taunton Street, but Belmont was the next suburb over.

The five of them could only just fit around the kitchen table. Elder Cowley's skin was flushed when he sat down, and after he'd begun he had to stop and lean over his manual, *A Systematic Programme for Teaching the Gospel*, to remind himself of the spiritual reference he was looking for. This studious pose didn't suit him. He was still growing into his bulk. Lorna had found herself following his progress when he passed by any neat arrangements, any objects that might tip or shatter. When he did gain mastery, there'd be nothing he couldn't do. He could win a gold medal.

Elder Miller, having less to keep track of, seemed to be in complete control of every limb and digit. Lorna could imagine him at a desk beside a telephone. While they waited he pointed at the jar of Vegemite on the bench. 'We don't have this,' he said. 'I see it everywhere. Is it malty?'

'Salty,' Lorna's mum said. 'It's made from yeast extract.'

'Is that right?' Elder Miller watched Elder Cowley flick through the pages.

'They work you hard, don't they?' her dad said. He would have been less likely to listen to the Elders if he thought they had it easy.

'Here it is,' Elder Cowley said. 'Ephesians four. Christ appointed apostles, prophets, evangelists, pastors and teachers.' His lips were full like pillows, almost too full, as though they'd be cumbersome to eat and speak with. 'We're talking about man's need for authority, not just in the heavens but here on Earth, flesh and bones. There are apostles among us right now. Who else was flesh and bones, from our last discussion?'

'God and Jesus,' Lorna said. The Mormon lessons blended the Bible stories with the real world. They were living in their own Bible now—they didn't have to wait until they were in heaven. 'Only the Holy Ghost is a spirit.'

'That's right,' said Elder Cowley. 'You've been listening.'

Elder Miller was nodding at Lorna as though he'd only just noticed she was there. 'Lorna would be the right age to supervise the children in our primary session,' he said. 'Has Sister Palmer asked you about that?'

When the lesson was over, the family grouped around the door to see the Elders out. Lorna's mum pulled back the curtain and peered outside. 'Are you sure you'll be all right? I don't like sending you back out into this rain.'

'We'll be fine.' Elder Miller wouldn't be diverted from putting his coat back on.

Her mum hadn't quite got it out of her system. 'I'd be tempted to get the camp beds out if I thought you'd stop here.'

Lorna glanced at Elder Cowley. He met her eye for a beat, then went back to putting his arm into the sleeve of his raincoat. Neil Cowley, that was his name. She was going to think of him as Neil from now on.

'Don't be silly,' her dad said. 'Let them get on with it.' He opened the door.

'See you on Sunday,' Elder Miller said.

It was her dad who dusted off birth certificates and visited registry offices, and who ordered their genealogical supplies from the church ('What's the difference between a *Handy Book for Genealogists* and a *Genealogy Handbook*?' he asked. 'The *Handbook* is cheaper,' Lorna's mum said.) He traced their lineage, including her mum's Scottish parents in Whangarei, all the way back to a drover from Jersey on her dad's side who came via New South Wales and who may have had criminal secrets but could still, in death, be baptised and saved so they could join him in eternity. The only hurdle was, none of their living relatives wanted to be baptised in the Church of Jesus Christ of Latter-day Saints.

Lorna's grandpa just shook his head and looked uncomfortable. He had a moustache and a gentle forward curve. In his cardigan, he looked like a bear. 'I can give you a copy of our gospel to take with you,' her mum said. 'There's a branch in Whangarei who would send someone over to visit.' She sat at the front of her chair the way Elder Cowley had, holding her back straight by pushing her hands into the seat on either side of her legs. Gran was a similar height to Grandpa but more imposing. She fixed her glare on Lorna, leading from the nose and brow. They were currently Presbyterians. 'What do you make of all this?' she asked. 'You're being a good girl and following along, are you?'

Lorna didn't know how to answer. People didn't usually ask her opinion. She thought Gran might understand better if she met the Elders and heard what they promised. The girls at school thought crossing the harbour to Auckland was the great beyond. They had no idea. Church magazines such as the *Relief Society* used words like 'fall' for autumn, and 'pavement' and 'drugstore'. The style of the drawings in the Mormon pamphlets was completely different. Jesus was stronger and more handsome.

'We met another family in the church,' Lorna said. 'Their daughter has been called to the States. She's going next year.'

Gran smiled for the first time since Lorna's mum had started talking. 'Nothing like a healthy dose of self-interest to keep you grounded,' she said. 'Have you heard of Short Creek?'

'They were fundamentalists,' Lorna's mum said. 'The church denounced them.'

'Well, don't believe everything you hear, but believe some things,' Gran said. 'I wouldn't bother trying to recruit any of our departed on this side of the family. They're happy where they are.'

Grandpa had been watching Lorna's dad. He tapped his tarry pipe on the side of the ashtray and sighed. Tobacco wasn't allowed in the Word of Wisdom either, but her mum had decided to make tea and put an ashtray out to start them off on a familiar footing. Lorna was probably the one who was most comforted. Her grandparents were the same as ever, right down to Grandpa's bitter smell. 'If you get some peace out of this, George,' he said, 'it will be worth it.'

Funny he should say that, Lorna thought. It had been ages since she'd been awoken by her dad's cries, muffled but urgent, and had opened her bedroom door. The hallway would be swamped in thick darkness and foreign, and her mum would be murmuring wordlessly from their room. She'd tended not to bother them with her own worries. Besides, chances were she would have forgotten by the time she woke up. Usually she would have; not always.

———

The morning Neil visited her during the primary session, the younger children were interpreting the Holy Trinity in crayon: one wanted to talk to Lorna non-stop, the others had their elbows splayed and their faces an inch away from the paper or their heads leaned in together, conspiring. Neil and Elder Miller were a pair, which meant they were supposed to be together all the time, but Neil was alone that day, without the other's mild, specky influence. 'Ignore me,' he said, but it wasn't easy when he placed a chair down beside her amongst the unselfconscious bodies, swinging feet, wet tongues fixed in the corners of mouths, fingers twisting hair. His knees stuck up from the child's seat he was on and Lorna could see the shapes of his thighs through his suit trousers, hard versus her soft. The girl who had been chattering at her picked up a crayon and put on a mask of concentration. From time to time a car would rumble past outside, the sound carried through high windows. 'Where's your picture?' Neil asked her.

'I'm helping them.'

'I'll give it a try.' He rummaged in the crayon box and came out with an orange. He drew three circles and began shading them in. 'You only need to create the right feeling,' he said. 'It can be symbolic.' She watched him add pulsating rays that covered the whole page. She was glad she hadn't started a picture after all. It would have been mediocre. She didn't know how to respond to this level of attention except to try to breathe evenly, which wasn't easy, and hope the air would travel smoothly through the thumping in her chest. 'Hey,' he said. 'What month were you born?'

'November,' she said.

'"November." That accent is so cute.' She thought, What accent? He'd had ample opportunity to comment on it before.

He was acting different. He took a chapbook out of his pocket and flicked to the page he wanted. 'November,' he said, 'which is the same as my brother. Says here your stone is topaz and your flower is—' he had to sound it out—'chrys-an-the-mum. What's that?'

'It's like a dahlia,' she said, but he didn't show any signs of knowing what one of those was either. She'd been worried that he might ask a gospel question, but God hadn't come up.

'Do you know what colour a topaz is?' he asked.

'It's yellow.' She had a doll called Topaz.

'Right!' He held out the open book to show her the picture. 'That's Topaz Mountain, in Utah, where they mine for them. You might go there one day.'

'Does this look like Godhead?' Wiremu had brought his drawing over to show Lorna. He looked sceptical as usual. What he'd drawn resembled Cerberus, from her Greek Myths and Legends unit. She angled it so Neil could see it.

'Holy moly,' he said.

'The Father, Son and Spirit seem quite angry,' Lorna said.

'I'll help you with it,' Neil said. Wiremu pointed his questioning gaze at Lorna. She nodded encouragement and handed the drawing to Neil.

'We teach that God, Jesus and the Holy Spirit are three separate and distinct personages,' Neil said, reaching for the crayons. 'We might have to perform surgery here.'

Later, too late, Lorna found out that Neil's father had shipped him over from Salt Lake City to get him away from something. In the meantime he leaned in towards her and spoke very quietly. 'Have you ever heard of necking?' She hadn't. It sounded as though it could have something to do with poultry. He was so close to her, though, and his voice was so low, that she sensed the kind of thing it might be.

Walking back from lunch, Lorna's mum told them that Barbara, whose husband had the goitre, had seen the branch president, Elder Palmer, with his wife in their car that morning and that she, Sister Palmer, had been primping in her hand mirror like a debutante. Barbara was a gossip, her dad said. He had begun to dress more smartly in recent months and wore a shirt and sports jacket more often, whereas her mum wore less lipstick and rouge than before. In particular, women had to guard against the wrong kind of attention. What Lorna had noticed, though, was that the most senior Sisters were the ones who took the most care over their appearance. They might be more confident about where the line was. Sister Palmer, who led the Mia Maids group for fourteen- and fifteen-year-olds, told the girls later the same day that God would choose a husband for each of them. Just sit tight and wait. He would tell the men. They would know, and they would come looking.

She began her investigation of necking at school, while sitting out basketball practice at the side of the court. Her mum had disapproved of the way the girls' skirts flew around ever since the high school 'she-demons' in Christchurch had murdered one of their mothers. The case was in all the newspapers and on the radio, but she wouldn't have it mentioned in the house. Lorna was reading a story in the *Improvement Era* about Marsha, who was an Honour Bee, and how she refused when Thad offered her alcohol. No one would ever be called Thad in New Zealand, holy or unholy, and no one outside their branch would understand about being an Honour Bee.

Through the scuffing of shoes on concrete, the teacher

blew her whistle. 'Aggressive play, Anne Fletcher.' The scuffing stopped, and a few moments later the bench shifted as Anne Fletcher sat down beside Lorna. On the field behind the court, a line of soccer boys stopped running, touched the ground, and ran back the other way. Lorna could sense Anne's face turned towards her. 'Do you have it bad, that time of the month?' Anne asked eventually.

'Sometimes,' Lorna replied. When she didn't say anything else, Anne sat back and faced forward. To her and her friends, Baptists were happy clappies, Germans were Jerrys, and Catholics were tolerated because there were so many. For Lorna's part, she knew Anne was exposed to all manner of corrupting influences. That's what people at church said about families that weren't religious. On the other hand, if she was willing to discuss periods, she might discuss other things. The players had formed a semi-circle to practise their shooting. The ball bounced off the hoop over and over again, every now and then juddering through.

'You're a Mormon aren't you?' Anne said. 'That's the American one, isn't it? Are there Americans in your church?'

'Quite a few, the missionaries are.'

'Do they have a lot of wives? That's Mormons, isn't it?' A seagull on a rubbish bin watched with its empty stare or didn't watch, impossible to tell.

'Only a few did,' Lorna said. 'Last century.' Anne's wide, freckled face wasn't hostile. If anything, she seemed curious, even eager. Lorna decided to risk it. Anne might tell her friends, but there was nothing Lorna could do about that. She leaned in and lowered her voice.

'Do you know what necking is?'

'Are you kidding?' She said it loud enough to scare the

seagull away. The teacher on the court turned towards them, then back again. She must have decided Anne was a lost cause. 'Why?'

Lorna didn't answer her.

'It's kissing and that,' Anne whispered, and Lorna felt what she thought might be the blessing of the Holy Spirit, like a rubber band pulled back in her stomach.

Taunton Street ran across three squares on the map Lorna had taken from the shelf above the serving hatch at home. Her mum thought she was at the library. The school bus had run parallel to Taunton for more than two years, but as soon as she got off at the unfamiliar stop and turned the corner away from Lake Road it was as though she'd entered a different realm, where the ground tilted, the green-sprouting trees were taller than theirs and there were no front walls or hedges or fences, just broad lawns open to her and anyone who happened to go past. Here, she was under a nothing-grey dome of sky, smack-bang in the outside world for anyone to see. Neil and Elder Miller could be behind her or across the road, and what would she say if she bumped into them? It might be God warning her off, that rush inside her when she saw the number two on a letterbox, not a sudden jolt but something that gripped and held her, pumping her heart harder. The Elders stayed at number four. She would have thought God would understand: the end result would be the same, wouldn't it, whether or not she sat tight and waited for something to happen? In her satchel was an envelope addressed to Neil and inside that was a beach stone, which had been sitting on her windowsill since she was little. Its orange grain had dulled now, and of course she knew it wasn't topaz, but there were seer stones in the Book of Mormon, and this one might prophesise something.

★

The Sunday it happened, Elder Palmer opened the door to the room where the Mia Maids were waiting and told them Sister Palmer was not able to lead the session. He had brought them the literature, he said. He knew they were plenty mature enough to use the time well, reading. Behind his square glasses, his eyes swept back and forth across them, not landing anywhere, perhaps expecting more of a response than he got. He seemed just as uncomfortable performing this errand as they were surprised to see him. The impression he left behind was enough to keep their lips zipped for a while. Of the books in the box, Lorna put aside *The Celestial Light* and *Women in the Kingdom of God* and reached one she hadn't been expecting to see, *A Systematic Programme for Teaching the Gospel*. The first chapter, 'Making the Contact', gave detailed instructions on how to conduct a house call. 'You should smile as the contact opens the door,' it said. 'Make your delivery smooth.' 'The first few seconds at the door will generally determine whether you get in or not.' God had chosen the Elders to teach His word, that was the understanding, but why had He given them a handbook that could have been devised for a door-to-door salesman?

The other two Mia Maids had given up on their reading and were chatting. Lorna excused herself and stepped out into the hallway that ran along the side of the building. All of the lines in the corridor were straight: window frames, blinds, ceiling, walls, floor, but they couldn't contain the sun and wind. Shadows were bursting in and upsetting the order.

Stripes and blobs bounced across the walls, and, when she pressed a hand against the plaster in their path, over her. If God was all powerful, He had done all of the interesting stuff way back before the Bible was written. Nothing like a flood that covered the earth would happen now. Lorna was still watching the shadows flare and scatter when one of the doors at the end of the hallway sucked air in as it was pushed open. She rushed for the door handle to avoid being seen. 'Wait,' a voice said. It shouldn't have been him, not in the real world, not unless it was divine intervention or a test.

'Hey there,' Neil said. 'Are you okay?' He stopped so near to Lorna that she had to lift her head or speak to a wall of chest. 'You look a bit pale. Where are those rosy cheeks?'

'I just needed some fresh air,' she said.

Neil swung the door open. Lorna had never been in this room before. It had a sink and bench on one side and a chair beside a divan on the other. There were no windows, nothing to look at, nothing to notice except a faint smell of empty drain. He sat on the chair and pointed to the divan for Lorna. They were alone; he was ignoring the rules for her sake. 'Is this fresh enough?' He smiled, and there was an admission in it, a smile not everyone would see from a man not everyone would know.

'Yeah, it's good,' she said. They might have been chosen to be together. He might be planning to let her in on it, and that might involve necking. She hadn't anticipated what would actually happen, that he would rest his hand around her leg, just above her knee, an intimacy that pinged the rubber band in her stomach.

'I wish I didn't have to rush this,' he said. 'I wanted to tell you in person that our mission here is almost over.' He put the other hand in his pocket. Surely not a ring. No, he brought out the stone she had left in their letterbox. 'Do your parents know you came all the way over to the house?' he asked.

Something was odd. The hand on her leg was out of sync. The more time she spent with him face to face, the more he differed from the version she nurtured in her mind the rest of the time. This Neil smiled differently, said different things. If he was leaving, that meant the end, and sure disappointment. Yet there they were. No, her parents didn't know. She shook her head.

'I didn't think so. Better that they don't.' Those were the words. His fingers weren't listening to the words. His fingers were performing their own manoeuvres, further up her leg. 'Hey, we haven't got much time left. I'll be leaving in a week or two, and I don't know when I'll be back. Not without a reason, anyway.' The cold grey tiles underfoot, the tap behind him, to the left of his head. Neither suggested anything momentous was happening. 'We haven't got much time.' He said it again. 'There's something really important I want to talk to you about. Something about your future.'

She felt a pressure under her jaw, as though she were filling up from the feet, and whatever it was she was filling up with had reached that high. His lips might be too big for kissing. They would cover more than just her lips. They would cover some of the skin around her mouth too. Her face was turned up to him. But still he talked. And still the fingers stretched out and came to rest somewhere near the inside of her leg, and she thought, What has that got to do with anything? The sensation was difficult to ignore, ticklish and intrusive, but she overlooked it for the meantime.

So far, nothing about God, nothing about Him bringing them together.

'Maybe I could come back and take you away with me,' he said.

That was it. That was what she'd been waiting to hear. Of course he knew her. He'd been to their house heaps of times. She leaned over and kissed the part of him she could reach, which was the side of his jaw. His skin was smooth, of course, but close up she could see the pinpricks of hairs he had shaved off and smell his sweat. He let her do it, but he looked puzzled for a moment; this wasn't going according to his plan either, then he leaned down and kissed her. There was the thrill of being kissed, then there was the feeling of the kiss itself, which was not exactly enjoyable, which was wet and more mechanical than she'd imagined.

'We don't have much time.' He said it a third time, and the fingers that were pushing down on the bridge of fabric between her thighs disappeared, then reappeared above her knee again, but underneath her skirt. None of the snippets of romance she'd read in magazines or heard on the radio had mentioned hands on bare knees, or fumbling with zips, as his other hand was, in his lap. It was obvious from his posture, his eye-line, even the hand squeezing her leg, that as far as he was concerned this was where she should be directing her attention.

'You have stated that you are ministers. (Generally respected and acceptable.)' That was what *A Systematic Programme for Teaching the Gospel* said. 'You are clean, neat, and conservatively dressed.' Lorna's calling was only to take the primary session. Part of what she felt now was honoured that Neil would show her this raw, straining purpose, which was so undignified.

'I can join us in the eyes of God,' he said. 'I can say an invocation.'

★

A bumblebee buzzed in an azalea beside the back step. Lorna and her mum each had a peg apron sewn out of an old curtain. They set out on the path that crossed the lawn like a jetty until they reached the pontoon, where the pole for the washing line was set into the concrete. The day was humid, the clouds half dissolving. 'It won't dry in a hurry.' Her mum used her foot to set the brake on the trolley that held the laundry basket, and leaned on the frame. She eyed people like Gran did, but less directly, with her head angled to the side. She was doing it now, from under the brim of her gardening hat. Curls had escaped and stuck out at funny angles on either side of her face. 'Have you been sick?' Lorna had vomited onto the silver beet that morning; nothing but a sudden bolt of nausea and an overspill, done with so quickly she'd forgotten.

'I felt sick,' Lorna said. 'But I'm fine now.' She was focussed on the Rotary fair later that day. She knew she was getting a bit old for it, that it wouldn't be the same, but she wanted to go anyway, to come back with candyfloss fingers and ringing in her ears from the fairground organ. She'd need her mum to supervise.

'We only had corned beef last night. I did it the usual way.' Her mum's hand was cool on her forehead. 'Are you sure?'

'Yes.'

'Good, you can wash the silver beet.' She stood back and let Lorna push the trolley towards the back door to be helpful, but they never went to the fair.

The next morning, in the kitchen, streaky shadows of invisible heat flowed over the temperature dials on the back of the stove. Already the smell of toast on the rack was stirring Lorna's unreliable stomach to hunger. Her mum had heard her from outside the toilet door. 'Has anyone at school had a tummy bug?' she asked.

'No.' Lorna wondered if hiding things from her mum could make her vomit. It didn't occur to her that the cause might be tangible. They had gone to Warkworth, Neil and Elder Miller, on their bikes, then embarked on a passenger liner from Queen's Wharf. When bits and pieces came back to her, there was no one to attest to anything.

'Not yet. Not your parents, not Elder Palmer. Not yet.'

It wasn't her parents who discovered their secret first, or Elder Palmer. It was the doctor, who listened to Lorna's symptoms with two fingers tapping his chair's armrest, staring into an empty upper corner of the room while her mum turned her ring around on her finger. 'Mrs Vardy, I would like to speak to Lorna alone for a few moments.'

'I would prefer to stay.' If the doctor heard the edge of alarm in her tone, he ignored it.

'All the same,' he said. Lorna could have been five not fifteen, her mum was so reluctant to stand up, but there was nothing more to say. He had the authority to issue orders, thanks to his jacket and tie and the framed degree on the wall.

'Yes doctor.' Her mum winced as she straightened. Rather than take pity on her, the doctor waited for the door to click shut.

'Have you been menstruating regularly?' he asked.

For some reason Lorna's gaze was stuck on the pencil sharpener beside his arm, which was the kind they had at school, with a handle and jaws. There was still a pencil in it, as though they'd interrupted him. After they left he would go back to his sharpening.

'I'm not sure,' she said. She had never been regular. 'I haven't had it for a while.' Now. This was the moment when she remembered the rabbits in biology. From then on, everything sped up.

'Have you had sexual relations?'

'Yes.'

'Were you forced?'

'By virtue of the holy priesthood, I pronounce us . . .'

'No.' She wasn't shocked or dismayed, at first. It was as though she'd been pulled up onto a plateau at the last minute. She was watching the storm descend on someone else. That couldn't be her down there in her school lace-ups and school skirt, which had another inch to be let out and no more, in case she planned to do any more growing, her mum had told her.

'What's your connection to this person? How long have you been in the relationship?'

He had padded over to lock the door in his shirt and singlet. His skin was paler underneath his clothes, pale against the nest of dark hair. 'Lift your hips up.' She had watched him slip her underwear down her legs and over her feet, watched to find out what he was going to do.

———

'Since Sunday the twenty-ninth of August,' she said.

'Did you use contraception: joeys, a cap?'

Even words couldn't be relied on to mean what she thought. 'I don't know.'

'Haven't you had health education classes? Come on now, you're going to have to be brave.'

'My mother wouldn't let me go.'

He nodded and pushed a box of tissues towards her. 'I'll have the nurse take a urine sample, but from what you've told me Lorna, I think it's possible that you're going to have a baby. Since you are under the age of sixteen, this boy or man has broken the law.'

'What if we're married?'

'You can't be married,' he said. 'You're not old enough. You had better ask your mother back in.'

Her mum held the strap of her handbag in her hand rather than over her shoulder and walked faster than usual, causing it to swing back and forth, come just short of whacking her on the shins. She was wearing a suit jacket she had owned for as long as Lorna could remember, since before her dad had got back perhaps, when it was just the two of them. While they had the street to themselves she fired off only beginnings: 'What have you—' 'How could he—' She stopped as they got nearer to the shops. Lorna tried to see their familiar surroundings through the eyes of someone who was having a baby—advertisements on the sides of rubbish bins, the zebra crossing pole, glimpses of the water—but they were all the same as ever. The thought of herself and Neil as a mother and a father was too strange. Impossibilities had taken over. After the butcher's her mum didn't speak to her at all.

When her dad got home he hung his jacket up beside the door and went down the hallway to change out of his overalls, same as ever. From the floor in the lounge Lorna watched her mum move around the table laying out knives and forks on their weekday tablecloth, which was printed with a map of Taupo from a trip Lorna didn't remember. She did it gingerly, without reaching out or leaning over. When Lorna's dad came back wearing his fresh shirt and said, 'Something smells good,' her mum only paused for a moment to receive his kiss before going back for the condiments caddy, slotting in the salt and pepper and sauce bottles even slower than usual, and Lorna realised she wasn't the only one who was reluctant. Her dad sat down in his chair. He would be looking forward to putting his feet up and listening to the news. If her mum didn't say something soon he would turn the radio on. She had made it as far as the table with the caddy. 'Go to your room, Lorna.' Lorna got up. She avoided looking at her dad on her way past.

They couldn't get married until Lorna was sixteen. She might have to go and live in America, get married in America, even. It wouldn't be that kind of wedding, her dad told her. What kind? she'd asked. The kind to get excited about, he said. She counted the dimples in the ceiling tiles in Elder Palmer's living room and waited for a summons. On the table in front of her were issues of the New Zealand church's magazine, *Te Karere*, and a Little Golden Book. She flicked through *Te Karere* to find the quick quips. She read: 'The best way to get rid of a noise in your car is to let her drive herself' and 'Ninety percent of nervousness is just inflammation of the ego'. She put it back, picked up the Little

Golden Book and read about Betty the Blue Jay quietly, in suspense and oblivious, while next door Elder Palmer told her parents that a girl who was capable of allowing a man carnal knowledge of her was more than capable of lying about it. He did not care to know with whom she had broken the law of chastity but he was confident it was not Elder Cowley, who had a strong testimony and who would be taking up a sports scholarship at Brigham Young University the following year. The president had to insist that Lorna absent herself from church activities, including sacrament meetings, until after the baby was born at least. Having been awakened, she would need to pray diligently for her soul and for guidance.

Neither of her parents spoke until her dad had pulled the car out onto the street. 'If not him, then who?' he said. Lorna didn't think he was addressing her. He rarely had since the news broke. He'd been going through his same routines but had seemed less relieved to arrive home after work and in more of a hurry to switch on the radio. Yellow lines rolled out beside them. Lorna had come to believe it was her destiny to go. A planeload of women from Holland had landed in Christchurch with their wedding dresses just the year before. At least she'd be going the other way, she thought, from somewhere less interesting to somewhere more interesting, where they had televisions and birds could be blue. She hadn't seen Neil before he left. At the party held for him and Elder Miller, he had winked at her, and that was all. Next stop, Port Adelaide.

'Have you been telling us the truth, Lorna?' her mum asked.

'What do you mean?' A gland seeped somewhere at the back of her jaw. 'Can we please pull over?'

'Not here,' her dad said.

'She'll be sick,' said her mum. The glare from the sky, the tarseal peeling off beneath them: Lorna tried not to alight on any one sensation. By resetting her sight-line every second, by constant distraction, she could delay long enough for her dad to pull in outside a row of shops, where a woman in a blue dress and a delivery man turned away while she vomited beside the car.

Jim

The lights go down. Music comes in: big drums and low strings. No more chattering, it says, they've entered a realm of utmost bloody seriousness, but the hypnotist does nothing more than walk onstage. Ten races they could have bet on instead. The man's hair is slick with bloody Brylcreem.

The Great Kincaid. They're always 'The Great' or 'The Amazing' something. 'The Great Brooks' doesn't have quite the same effect. Besides, Jim wouldn't grow one of those beards, not if it turned Jane Russell into a housecat on heat. He has his limits.

'Press your hands together,' Kincaid says to the audience. 'Keep them there.' One of Jim's mates—the one who convinced them to go—seems to be battling, right hand against left, so bloody hard is he concentrating. The veins in his arms pop out. The other mate lights a cigarette. Jim starts with his hands clasped (he's paid for a show), but the barber he went to that morning let hair clippings fall down the back of his neck and now he needs to scratch himself. The train carriage was hot, the open windows letting an even hotter wind through. Their mate who made all the effort looks as though his budgie has died when, on the count of five, his hands drift apart.

Kincaid picks his six joiners, his six good sorts, and he puts them on chairs in the stage-lights, facing sideways. Two of the girls are good-looking, quite some profiles they've got. A waiting hush settles over the hall. The anticipation's heavy enough to smother coughs and squealing chair legs. Jim stares into the glow.

'I'll face my subjects and not the audience when I speak my directives,' says the Grand Poo-Bah, 'for fear of putting any of you into a dangerous unguided sleep state. Now, relax.' His precautions count for nought. Jim hasn't eaten recently, not since pies in Balclutha, and, as it turns out, drinking three bottles fast without any tea then sitting in a dark room is about his limit before he starts to feel just the slightest bit drowsy. On being told to relax, despite his not being inclined to listen to anything this suspected nancy might have to say, the effort to keep his eyes open is too much. When Kincaid announces, 'You are sinking into a deep, restful sleep,' it's true in at least one case. The mate nearest Jim nudges the other.

Later, Jim and his mates will pile flesh onto this story in the same areas, expand on what the hypnotist was wearing, his spiel, how fruity he was and the physical merits of his female subjects. They might embellish it with an extra flourish of facial hair on Kincaid or a loud snore from Jim at the end.

In a popular version Jim will take to his feet with the volunteers on stage and jerk at the air, clucking. They'll all eventually contradict each other on the details. As time passes, though, it will hardly matter; they won't see each other anymore, they'll even forget where they were and who they were with. Jim himself will sometimes wonder if the hypnotist planted something in his mind that has stayed with him and held him back.

Then again, it's just a yarn. No need to come over all po-faced.

Katherine

By the time Katherine introduced the question-and-answer session she had been standing for forty-five minutes and was looking forward to taking her place at the table nearest the dais, with the treasurer and president of the Women's Round Table Club. First to the microphone was a radio announcer. 'Were there any medical emergencies while the Bells were on the island?' she asked.

'Yes, certainly they hurt themselves and got sick,' Katherine said. 'And Frederica Bell gave birth to several children there.'

Next, 'How did they cope with the loneliness and isolation?'

'During the day they were working,' Katherine said. 'In the evening they read and sang together.'

She was somewhat surprised at the negative line of questioning. Suffering wasn't all they did. She was there to promote her new book, *The Crusoes of Sunday Island*, 'the true nineteenth-century adventures of the Bell family in the Kermadecs'. Once she would have been relating her own travels, but she hadn't been overseas for years. The wrinkled skin of her hands gripping her notes, the necessity to hold them closer to her eyes than in the past, testified to that.

An elderly woman approached the microphone. 'My husband was the High Commissioner in Tonga from 1907 to 1912,' she said. 'Certain members of the British Consul remembered Bell then.' She spoke with a slight quaver. 'He had died by the time we got there, but he lived until he was ninety. It just goes to show where all these new gadgets and appliances get you.' The last sentence was delivered in the same tone as those preceding it, a statement of fact. As it happened Katherine agreed with her. She had rarely met a soul as hale as Bessie Bell, the eldest daughter, who was nearing ninety herself now, but the club president had taken up an expectant stance beside the microphone.

'Thank you,' Katherine said. 'I'm told the family enjoyed remarkable health by and large throughout their lives, better than most.'

A keen chatter settled over the room. From time to time the tea trolley chimed in. The sandwiches were good: bread fresh, eggs fluffy and cucumber crisp. 'Who are you visiting these days?' she asked the president. She watched a platter being lifted away from their table with two egg and chive still on it.

'We still visit the psychiatric hospitals,' the president said, 'and the knitting groups are still doing hats and scarves.' The window behind them lit a fuzz of tiny hairs on her cheek. The same groups had knitted for the armed forces. A few particularly unfortunate men might have received a hat while serving in France and a scarf at Seacliff or Sunnyside. 'I hear they have a new superintendent on Rotoroa Island,' she said. Katherine was donating her appearance fee to the alcoholics' home there. 'Apparently he has quite a rapport with the inmates—patients, they're called now.'

'I'm glad to hear it,' Katherine said.

'Are you going on any trips overseas soon, Miss Morton?' the treasurer asked. She was the only one of them wearing a hat, in the princess style with a veil.

'I don't have any business travelling at my age,' Katherine said. The president protested straight away, but the treasurer wouldn't be deterred. She had asked with something else in mind than wanting to know the answer.

'My husband and I are off to Samoa on the Coral Route next week,' the treasurer said.

'Are you?' Katherine said.

'My son works for a company that has a contract building schools there,' she said. Katherine saw future generations, her great nieces and nephews, waving at her through the little windows, not so very different from portholes, soaring into the atmosphere for cocktails at so many thousand feet.

'Excuse me, Miss Morton. I'm sorry to interrupt.' Behind Katherine was the diplomat's wife. A violet rinse gave her lined skin the look of porcelain. 'Harriet Radon,' she said.

'No bother at all,' Katherine said. 'Let's find you a chair.'

Mrs Radon spoke directly to Katherine, meaning to finish what she had started at the microphone. 'I think you might know the botanist and zoologist Dr Wallace,' she said. 'He visited Raoul.' She was gripping her legs lightly just above her knees.

Katherine looked down at her plate to think while the president and treasurer continued talking. 'I haven't met him, but we have corresponded,' she told Mrs Radon. 'One of my slides was a photograph of his; it shows the huts they built on their earlier expedition.' Wallace's handwriting had revealed a tremor, the visual equivalent to Mrs Radon's voice.

'We met him in Tonga after that expedition,' Mrs Radon said. 'He was an interesting man, but he was unwell that day. He told us in private that a rare type of dung beetle from Raoul had scuttled out of one of his bags after he arrived. Exhausted as he was, he had to chase it around the room and catch it before he could preserve it to be classified.'

Katherine laughed. 'A stowaway.'

'Yes.' The waver was more obvious after the effort of the anecdote. 'He was sunburnt. He had that look they get.' Katherine knew. Wiry and hollow-eyed.

'Mrs Radon, have you met everyone?' the president asked. Katherine was grateful. She couldn't remember the treasurer's name. 'Mrs Irving is flying to Samoa next week,' the president said.

'Is that so,' Mrs Radon said. 'Do they still use the Solents?'

'They've built landing strips now,' the treasurer said. 'The bigger airliners are much more comfortable.'

Mrs Radon paused to take a breath. 'I was a passenger on their maiden flight in 1951. We enjoyed landing on the water. We didn't mind how long it took.'

Katherine's route that morning had taken her past Freeman's Bay, which was deserted these days, save the diggers and dozers preparing an approach road for the new harbour bridge, which would take so many thousand more cars than the ferry could, and so much faster. They were building taller and taller buildings, aspiring to the heights of the bigger cities; while Katherine felt herself to be reducing in size, stooping, eating less.

One of her brothers, Alfred, had not lived long enough to see electrical appliances become common, or to marry and have children who would take them for granted. Alive, he had been an admirer of skies and a painter of landscapes, but her memories of him had become remote, counted in years instead of miles. Her last souvenir had arrived from Geneva with a Red Cross letterhead in French. It was a form letter. 'We are unable to give you any news regarding your ....' Someone else had handwritten '*brother—Staff Capt. A.B. Morton*'. A higher-up must have deemed this the most efficient system, but it wasn't fool-proof, for nearer the bottom of the letter was an omission: 'Should anything definite about your .... reach us, we shall let you know without delay.' A gap was what he was reduced to and was what he remained; an absence, filled by reminiscences and occasionally by dark conjecture about his last moments.

'I'd better go back for my cake,' Mrs Radon said. She rose to her feet slowly. They must have been almost contemporaries, and Katherine wouldn't have minded knowing what injury or ailment had caused her movement to be compromised as it was, but she could hardly ask.

'Don't miss out,' Katherine said.

'Oh I don't intend to.'

The subject of Katherine's final travel lecture had been Louisiana, USA. When she'd come to write it, her notes had amounted to little more than a jumble of impressions, and her photographs weren't much better. The most useful was of a Cajun woman posed before her houseboat. Using her as the starting point, Katherine had been able to trace the origins of the Arcadians, quote Longfellow's *Evangeline* and describe some of the distinguishing features of Cajun culture. Another of her photographs was of two Negro mechanics seated on log stools, each with a rag in his hand and a box of engine parts at his feet. One of the men was significantly older, might have been the father of the other, and they had demonstrated a kind of watchful ease. She'd thought of Moses at the time. *Keep thy soul diligently, lest thou forget the things which thine eyes have seen . . . but teach them thy sons, and thy sons' sons.* Theirs was a more Old Testament society than her own, and weren't those Negro churches vibrant, or so she had been told.

She had been reminded when she developed the film of the befuddlement the young man had caused her at the time: the perfect sheen of the arm hanging down off his knee, oil can dangling from his finger. They had waited obligingly while she took the photograph, and although they had not smiled for the camera, they'd returned her grin when she thanked them and said goodbye.

She hadn't drawn particular attention to the young man in her lecture. In fact, while this slide was up, what had been high spirits among her listeners at the Lewis Eady Hall had drained out and had never quite returned. The Negro neighbourhood was known as Freeland, she had explained. The civic centre was still segregated. 'Separate but equal' was the slogan. In the queues at drinking fountains, coffee shops and post offices, everything except the skin was the same: the clothes and shoes, the range of ages, the bags slung over shoulders. She had decided not to give the talk again.

Her memories of the place shimmered and shifted. She couldn't reflect on images that had not resolved.

She had been invited there by Marcia, a children's writer she'd interviewed for the *Herald* and a member of the National League of American Pen Women, Louisiana Branch. The lecture she'd presented there, in the New Iberia parish hall, with a brand new air-conditioning machine buzzing in the background, was on the scenic wonders of New Zealand. Her American counterparts, most in their sixties, had been enthralled, either by the chiselled peaks of the Southern Alps or by the coolness of the room and the padded seats. Against their twangy accent her vowels were dull and unvarnished. 'New Zealand's main industry is agriculture,' she told them. 'In land area, we are comparable to the United Kingdom or Italy, but we were settled by Europeans not much more than a hundred years ago.' In handling the slides she had left a magnified thumb print off the Kapiti Coast. 'Next please.'

Take on one hand the port of New Orleans: at the edge of a continent, vast land instead of ocean. 'Worship and fish-fry' on a church billboard. The piping of a calliope from a steamboat, which carried for blocks, into a district where a party had taken hold and continued indefinitely for days, months, years and decades. Compare it to the unpopulated beech forests of home, rivers over rocks, spikes of matagouri bushes in the clearings, a glimpsed farmhouse with smoke drifting from the chimney; or Cape Reinga, a ridgeline with the Tasman Sea on one side and the Pacific Ocean on the other, falling away in cliffs and sand dunes. Even if life on the bayous and swamps of Louisiana was sleepier than the port had been, she and her audience were hardly likely to relate to each other. Marcia and her husband lived on an avenue of houses in the Greek Revival style, where the shade was sweet from scented blooms, the linen was crisp and the two Negro maids used their own stairs at the back.

'Could we have a look at your natives with their huts again?' The woman with button-like features had spoken up during the question-and-answer session.

'Slide fourteen please,' Katherine said. She waited until the image appeared on the screen. 'The Maori give wonderful cultural performances. They call their songs *waiata*.'

The woman had nodded. 'Our Negroes are good singers too. They call theirs spirituals.'

'Blues,' someone put in, 'jazz.'

'Those too,' the first woman said.

Jim

It was the light that woke him, so clear and unimpeded. Sounds were concerned only with themselves: birdcalls—a tui—then a wheel and footsteps over gravel. There'd be no barber's breakfast this morning. He jacked himself up on one elbow, saw a bucket, reached down for it.

He woke up again when the lieutenant came in. 'How are you feeling?
    'What have you got?'
    'Phenobarbital.'
    'Will it knock me out?'
    'Probably.'
    'I feel better for hearing that.'

———

Still later he got a packet of tobacco and papers and a box of matches. The hospital-issue towel and cake of soap on the end of the bed. The booklet entitled *Memoranda for Patients*.

If not inviting, his dorm bed should have been adequate. The sheets were white, Department of Health, turned down over a grey blanket. But Jim saw its infinite potential for contortion. He sat down and switched on the wireless. No Goons, nothing—it was outside permitted hours. He jigged his restless leg. No one was asleep yet. They were up and down the corridor, stomping. A record player or transistor was on somewhere, a conversation through the wall. A voice rose, peaked, then laughed. He lay back. A thump, as if someone or something had fallen to the ground, and a door closing. He dozed off and dreamed more of it, could have been asleep or awake. Hadn't been a good sleeper for years.

A mosquito drilled back and forth, near and then far off. Eventually he groped for his box of matches, struck one, aimed it towards the wick of his candle and inhaled the flare of sulphur. A flame stretched up and threw shadows into the corners. The mosquito fell silent.

He might be the only one awake on the island. Just this burrow of light he had carved out, and then nothing until Waiheke: corridors vacant, lumps in beds, chapel pews empty, snuffles and bumps in the barns. Only mice and possums, rats and cats and scuttling crabs still active, and him.

Lorna

Just another waiting room with a bay window, but there were none of the pamphlets or posters that were standard in doctors' surgeries. A hedge outside blocked the light and the view in from the footpath. Lorna's mum handed an envelope to the matron, hugged Lorna and dabbed at her eyes with her handkerchief. If Lorna could just survive the next four months or so life would start again, whatever it might consist of. Fruit stands, crowds on the beach, sleepy streets woken up by Cowboys and Indians: she'd missed them all that summer. Her only trip in their new car had been the journey there. She had sunk down into the back seat with her jacket bundled up in her lap, even for the ferry trip. She'd grown quite fond of her bump despite all the trouble; it was pleasant to rest her hands on. If her mum saw her she would frown and tap her wrist, as though Lorna were biting her fingernails or digging wax out of her ears. Her mum was always giving her funny looks. It was as though Lorna wasn't the person she'd assumed she was, and she couldn't be trusted to cooperate.

An age seemed to have gone by since Neil and Elder Miller's bikes had leant up against the fence that first time, since Wiremu had drawn his fangy Godhead.

'We'll look after Lorna.' The matron stood still, waiting, with the envelope in her hand. She didn't finger any buttons or fold and unfold her arms; that was for people like Lorna who had less control over themselves, and people like her mum who had raised wayward daughters.

Inside, the Sunflower Home was carpeted and furnished as a family home would be, but expanded and elongated, and the homeliness stretched thin too, the colours faded and the carpets worn. The whole ground floor was a glorified waiting room, equipped for an extra-long wait. In the air was a blend of cleaning fluids and the musk of girls living together, and sometimes, from upstairs, a kind of warmth generated by the mothers and babies. This was where the roughest girls from school ended up, the ones no one looked kindly on. A pair of gloves went missing the first week Lorna was there. The most intimidating of the residents leaned on the walls in the hallway outside their bedrooms, glaring, while they were searched. 'These rooms are disgraceful,' the matron said, coming out of one. 'Those who live like animals will behave like animals.' The gloves were later found in the back garden, dirty and dew-damp.

They lined up on seats in the recreation room one night to watch *Education for Childbirth*. The retractable screen was stuck and the caretaker had gone home, so the dorm sister had to point the lens at the wall instead. 'Not all of this will apply to you girls,' she told them from behind the projector, 'but it contains a lot of useful information.' Lorna was ready to be appalled. After all, there were hospital wards upstairs. They weren't at a girl scouts' jamboree.

The husband in the film checked the days off on his calendar, then ran ahead to the car to put a suitcase in the boot and open the passenger door, flapping around the still serene mother-to-be. After she arrived at the hospital she was tucked up between white sheets, or in this case white with faintly embossed leaves from the wallpaper. The narrator's voice was a man's, low, slow and reassuring. 'Remember to relax during your contractions,' he said. 'If you let yourself get too anxious, the muscles in your abdomen will tense up, making it more difficult for your baby to be born.' When the woman in the film had a contraction, she looked up from her knitting as though she could hear a train going past.

'Are they sure that's a baby and not a fart?' a voice murmured. Lorna turned to look behind her. The girl who'd spoken looked a few years older than her, though she was smaller and elfin. She must be one of the mothers. Lorna hadn't seen her before.

'Thank you Colleen, the rest of us would like to watch,' the sister said.

On the wall the father-to-be departed the scene to buy cigars and chocolates for the office, and before long his wife was wheeled on a gurney into a delivery suite, where she pulled faces and pushed her baby out, though the camera showed only her top half, the nurse dabbing at her forehead with a towelette. When it was all over, and the new parents were leaning over their baby admiring its toes, a message in text came up. 'The film you have seen was an average, normal birth. There may be some slight variation from it as far as you are concerned.' Colleen snorted and set off everyone else tittering.

'All right, all right,' the dorm sister said. 'The anatomical descriptions were accurate. Colleen, I don't know why you're here.'

Colleen was nursing a baby she had named Belle while she waited for her to be adopted. Her parents would kill her if they knew. Her husband was a no-hoper, she told Lorna. They already had a son. She'd had to leave him behind with cousins. Lorna's mum had told her she couldn't make friends with the girls from the home, but one afternoon while they were on kitchen duty Lorna told Colleen that the father of her baby lived in America, and that after the baby was adopted she might be sent on a mission there herself.

Two loosely corkscrewed strips of potato skin, each about two feet long, lay on the bench; Colleen had challenged her to a competition to see who could peel the longest, and won. In such a large kitchen, they were children themselves.

'If you're so religious, why did you do it with him?' Colleen asked.

'I thought we'd get married,' Lorna said. 'We already were, symbolically.'

'But the sex wasn't symbolic.' Colleen cut a potato in half and dropped it over the high wall of the aluminium pot. 'Do you think he'd done it before?'

'I never thought about it.'

'You don't think about much, do you?' she said, but she and Lorna were in the same predicament. She picked up the potato nearest to her, saw how knobbly it was and chose another.

'So it was a holiday romance?'

'He was on a mission, not on holiday.'

'You know what I mean: he was overseas, only here for a short time, you fell for each other . . .'

'It did happen quite suddenly,' Lorna said.

'Like a lightning strike. Does he definitely know you're having a baby?' Colleen clutched her arm. 'Oh my God—he might be over there in his blue jeans, chewing gum, pining for you.'

Lorna was relieved someone else thought so too.

'Where did you do it?' Colleen asked.

She probably shouldn't tell her. 'The sick bay.'

'Love-sick!' Neither of them had seen the matron come in.

'Are you girls getting the vegetables ready or chatter-boxing?' she asked. It didn't matter how old you were, you were either a member of the staff or you were a girl.

'Both,' Colleen told her.

Joan from the farm was fourteen. If Lorna were cattle, she'd be a springing heifer, that's what Joan told her when she had only a month to go. They were brushing their teeth in their nightgowns. 'For a while after you give birth you'll still be a heifer, then you'll be a cow.'

Joan was curvy for her age. Even without the baby she would have stood out from the others in her year. With the baby, there was something off straight away, like a kid in the primmers smoking or a boy bent over a walking stick, which could also happen of course, some people got struck down. The oldest girl at Sunflower was at least thirty, and was said to have stalked the footpath in the dead of night committing heinous sins. She read tea leaves, pointing out the patterns with perfectly painted fingernails.

Lorna spat in the sink. 'Would the matron be a cow?' she asked.

'Not if she hasn't had any children.' Joan zipped up her toiletry bag. It was larger than Lorna's and made of a heavier fabric. 'She'd still be a heifer I think. I don't know if there's a word for old cows that haven't given birth. They'd get eaten.' She grinned from her frilly collar, a housewife in miniature. They stood before the lines of tiny mirrors and sinks, delaying going to bed. 'She wouldn't be as tough as some,' Joan said, as though to start them off again. Lorna didn't like being alone either, but it was doors closed at nine.

Outside her bedroom window, beyond the cotton, lace and glass, across the lawn and on the other side of the back wall, would be traffic and people walking home. Lorna needed a distraction from the worst of the rumours that went around, about bloodbaths, and deformed or blue babies. She wasn't allowed a radio, so she had to make do with what was already there, which wasn't much. Her parents had given her prayer books she'd hardly opened, except to leaf through the tissue pages with their gold edging and study the illustrations at the beginning, Nephi and his people reaching the promised land, Moroni burying the Nephite record. The pictures looked exaggerated to her now, as though all the men in biblical times had done weightlifting. The girls had each been given a ring binder to file homecraft lessons in— patterns and recipes, diagrams of nappy folding and hygiene guidelines—even if most of them didn't need to know how to raise a baby yet because they wouldn't be raising theirs. They were always being warned off worrying about the birth (ninety percent of nervousness was inflammation of the ego), but sometimes Lorna couldn't sleep. She wondered what would happen if she fainted. She wondered what would happen if she couldn't push the baby out. The bump was elbowing and kicking her now. She tried to imagine what it was like in there, submerged in a dark sack, sometimes red when the light came through, whether the baby felt scared or didn't know any better.

She could divert herself with the well-creased book Colleen had told her to hide under her mattress, *Safari Passion*, which started the same way as a lot of the stories she was used to, with a young woman facing temptations and dilemmas, but which was developing differently already; the leading man's lips had crushed down on hers no more than a few chapters in. There was always an envelope on the desk, addressed with her mum's jerky lines and loops, awaiting a response.

Lorna and her mum had been rehanging curtains one morning after the school term had finished when her mum eased herself down off the chair. Despite the way she moved to protect her back, testing before she committed, she didn't really look old, not as old as most mothers. She said, 'When I had you, my organs swelled up and I couldn't breathe. I couldn't have another baby.' Her letters warned Lorna to tell someone if her hands and feet got any bigger, but every couple of weeks the doctor had wrapped the cuff around Lorna's arm and declared her blood pressure 'tickety boo' before passing her over to the nurse and the familiar pinch in her arm for blood. They were moving, her mum had written in her latest letter. They had bought a house in Albany. That might have been the subject of the armchair summits Lorna had occasionally walked in on at home.

From thirty-five weeks onwards she had the crackling of a plastic sheet on her bed to look forward to each night, which turned out to be all for nought. She wasn't in bed or even in her room when her waters broke, she was with Colleen. Belle had been adopted, wasn't even Belle anymore, and Lorna was helping Colleen to pack her things, or at least watching her pack: a wall frieze, a row of pansies cut out of a housekeeping magazine, a Savon soap box she liked, and the pair of jacquard gloves recovered from the back garden. She hadn't cracked any jokes for a while. 'I was lucky with Belle,' she said. 'She was a looker. I knew someone would want her.'

Lorna felt like a cross between a punching bag and an overinflated balloon of stretched skin. Twice since she'd been there with Colleen she'd got sore with bad cramps. Then it happened, and the pad she was wearing didn't contain the fluid. Colleen didn't notice at first. When Lorna bent forwards, she looked down and realised.

'Oh my God.' Colleen smiled a gift of a smile at Lorna— a vote of confidence—and gave her the towel from her rail. 'For you. Don't worry about the floor, someone else will do it.'

Unlike the film, this was in colour, with red geraniums in a vase across the room and, outside, under a flat scab of cloud, the promise of blue sky. Instead of a husband, Colleen came and hugged Lorna in her bed. The doctor arrived to take her blood pressure, felt around her abdomen, lifted the sheet and her gown and exposed her to the air, looked at her down there. She turned her head and watched the night's rain, still dripping from the trees. A contraction started while he was there. 'All right, I know,' he said. 'Keep breathing, it's going to be all right.' His voice made her cry.

The nurses couldn't be so sympathetic, they weren't immune; they were in the trenches, fighting with her, the cycle of panic, pain and relief, panic, pain and relief, eventually more pain and less relief. They gave her pills in a paper cup, which didn't so much take the pain away as fade her surroundings, blend them with the agony in a blurred nightmare. The flare of the doctor's yellow tie against the white and stainless steel in the delivery suite (did he say 'get that vacuum cleaner out of here'?), no faces anymore, only masks; no flowers, only trolleys of instruments as though she were at the dentist but bigger and more of them and she opened her legs instead; and finally, when they had her lie back to place the mask over her face, a round lamp bent over on a craning arm. 'Keep breathing,' the nurse said. 'That's it, just breathe.' Then there was only waking in and out of tearing, searing pain that couldn't be right, must be a disaster, must be dying, impossible to know how many times. Only once did she manage to open her eyes and cry out at the group huddled in the range of her spread legs. The doctor looked up and she thought he was going to speak to her, but what he said was,

'Nurse.'

That was just what it felt like to have a baby. He was a boy, Lorna's baby, and he had been taken away by the time she woke up back in the room with the geraniums, too groggy to be relieved. She put a hand on her stomach and wondered at the transformation. It was dusk again, a premature twilight to her, when they finally brought him and laid him in her arms. He was red and his eyes were jammed shut and he was frowning so hard he could have been carrying the whole world's troubles, but his weight, insignificant at first then

53

more substantial the longer she held him, put her back up to full complement. His skin was sticky when she touched his cheek, his nose and his eyebrows, as though he still hadn't quite dried out. If she had been married, she would get to keep him, but he was going to be redistributed to someone more deserving.

Never mind that the matron said 'well done': they were going to take him away, when she knew him better than anyone. The pressure in her chest increased. She found it harder to breathe. If she didn't concentrate on drawing in the air, she might stop breathing altogether. She felt as though she might vomit. She looked down at the baby's angry face and tried to bring her thoughts back, but they whirled away from her, out of reach. She couldn't control it. In an unwelcome pulse of understanding she felt that her old joys had passed and that everything would be different now. If she didn't calm down she was bound for an institution, where she would sit in a room with locked windows and staff with huge arms.

'Lorna?' the matron said. Lorna stared at the baby's little fists, which were rigid with indignation, and wondered if they were right after all: she couldn't take care of him, she wasn't safe, but she didn't tell the matron that, not yet. She wanted him to stay.

'Take a few deep breaths,' the matron said. 'Come on.'

On the front of the booklet there had been a drawing of a rose in a circle. The text had begun, 'If intimacy leads to unhappy results . . .' A fresh start was best, it said. She'd written her name in her best joined-up handwriting underneath where her mum and dad had signed. She didn't have a signature.

Sleepy, that was all she could think at six in the morning when one of the nurse aides woke her and led her down the hallway, through a dim stillness. The room they entered was large and clean-shabby like the others. Cots lined one wall, and armchairs another; two were occupied by girls with their bundles of baby. So this was where the warmth originated, not respectable, but strong. In one of the cots was 'Baby Vardy', according to the name-tag on the frame. His face was still red and wrinkled and he blinked with blank grey eyes that didn't understand anything.

'Can I pick him up?' Lorna asked. The aide nodded. Lorna peeled back the covers, took hold of him around his middle and lifted his weight again, that dense body, helpless, with its legs and arms hanging.

'Come and sit down,' the aide said. 'See if he'll feed. Your nightie unbuttons around the front.' She busied herself checking the nappies of the other babies.

Lorna sat down in the empty armchair and used her free hand to get her nightdress open. He became more and more agitated, waving his mouth around, as she moved him into position. He took a while to make a seal. When he did she stared down at his feathered head, embarrassed by the sensation but pleased to be of some use.

They gave her injections for the next two days but peeing still hurt. Getting from lying down to sitting up hurt. Every morning a nurse came and unhooked the binder she was wearing around her middle, swabbed her between the legs and measured her from the top of her pubic hair to her belly button. When she needed to go to the toilet they pushed a bedpan between the sheets. It had been so long since she'd had herself to herself, it was hard to remember who she was before.

The first thing she thought of was her bedroom at home, which had always been hers, but she'd be going back to Albany and a house she'd never seen. She dreaded two things. Colleen had warned her about the stitches coming out, that was one. The other was the phone ringing, bright and insistent, in the matron's office, directly under the ward. That would be it, she thought, every time. That would be the call.

When the sun came out and shone warmth onto her covers, she got scratchy. She was alone in the ward, and bogged down from being in bed too long. When no one was around she snuck out of bed to catch a bird's-eye peek down into the empty back garden, which was like the lawn beside a library or war memorial, hardly ever occupied. Twice since she'd been at Sunflower a man had been escorted through the house and out the back door, where he'd been joined by one of the girls on a bench and had sat smoking with his sleeves rolled up. A group of the other girls had watched from a ground-floor window: two people staring at a birdbath wishing they'd done things differently.

Now all Lorna could see of the garden from the ward upstairs was grass, and branches full of browning leaves that obscured the bench and birdbath. Her baby would be gone by the time they fell. She stayed long enough to see two figures walk down the steps from the house. Once she had seen them she had to keep watching, because they were familiar. She recognised her mum and dad almost instantly, despite the odd angle. This is it, she thought. She got back into bed to wait for the matron, but the matron didn't come.

A full week went by before she was finally called to the matron's office. By that time she was able to get up and dress herself again. When she arrived she took in the details hungrily, anything to delay the inevitable news. Her mum and dad were there, sitting at a table near the door. Her mum was dressed up in a hat and her dad's haircut could only be a day or two old. They were holding hands. Lorna's seat didn't have a cushion. The room was long and thin. A heavy desk at the window end was surrounded by cupboards and shelves, some with keyholes.

'We thought it would be too dangerous for you to have another baby,' her mum said. 'We couldn't let your only baby be a stranger.' She leaned forward, her persuasive pose. 'By the time it was obvious you were all right, we'd got used to the idea.'

They'd even thought up a name, Isaac. Lorna hadn't got sick, she could have more children, but they wanted to raise him anyway.

'What about your back?' Lorna asked. 'What will we tell people?' There'd be no fresh start. Instead there'd be a lie that would grow with the baby, year after year. They'd all be in it together.

Her mum sat back. 'So you'd be happy to give him away?'

Her dad's voice was calm. 'We'll manage.' He was far off, beyond where she could get through to him. She had seen that look before.

The house in Albany was set back from the road, at the end of a long driveway. Lorna stayed behind in the back seat while her mum carried Isaac inside, sheltered by her dad's umbrella. All she could see of the new house in the dark was the outline, and patches of sills and eaves in the glow of the lights they switched on. She watched her mum, framed in the window of the front room, lower Isaac into the bassinette. When she pulled the curtains, Lorna focussed instead on the drops of water jittering and squirming on the windows, quivering and breaking off, more and more, always replenishing. The sound of the rain on the car roof was incredibly peaceful, made her feel as though she could be anyone in a car anywhere— anywhere it was raining, where rain was the only sound.

Her dad loomed out of the darkness and retreated towards the back of the car, but he didn't open the boot. He clicked open the door on the other side of Lorna, got in and clunked it closed. He didn't say anything at first, just seemed to listen with her, but the silence had changed. She looked at her hands, her nails trimmed as the sister had instructed. 'This way you can live your own happy and productive life,' he said. Just like that. She thought of the brickmaking plant where he was foreman, where productive meant a good yield of bricks stamped with Goode Brothers. 'You can't exactly look after him yourself, can you?'

'No.'

He put his hands on his knees and breathed out heavily. 'Do you feel better now?' Better now she'd had the baby or better now he'd spoken to her? Once he knew, he could get on with things. If only life was like that, either one thing or the other, and not just made up as you went along.

'What about church?' she asked.

'Let us worry about that.' He pulled the handle on his side and she did hers. The silence had been ruined anyway. She wasn't anyone, anywhere. She was herself, here. She was wearing pads in her bra. Her breasts ached.

Wet coats in the hallway. A kitchen ahead of her at the end of the hall, bedrooms off to the right. This house was older, with darker carpet. Fug of steam from the kettle. The milk powder foamed when her mum poured on boiling water, a claggy smell. 'Can I help?' she asked.

'You go on to bed,' her mum said. 'Get some rest.'

Her bed was made up and her old dressing table was there, the key that had always hung on a string around the frame that held the mirror. She had never known what it was for. She changed out of her clothes and padded into their room to look down at Isaac, then she went back, dug in under the covers and spent half the night waking to doors and cupboards and, later, mewling, her breasts leaking, bedsprings and floorboards. She dreamed of before, before Neil and Isaac, on Takapuna Beach. Someone was watching her (from behind or above, she didn't know), but she couldn't help heaping the warm sand into her lap, heaping it up and patting it down into the shape of Rangitoto, and watching what happened when she lifted her hips, watching it crack and slide. When she lay back in the sand, muted shouts and squeals of the other bathers—a child somewhere, a baby. Later, she would have to tip the sand out of the gusset of her swimsuit and find it in her ears, but those were practical considerations, waking thoughts, and they shifted her. She was a long way from the beach. Eventually she opened her eyes to a window at a new angle, curtains covered in a complex floral fabric, an unfamiliar room and no clock beside the bed, as disorientating as the dream had been but solid and distinct. She flicked her blankets back and swung her legs around. What got her up was the thought of seeing Isaac.

Jim

Jim and the rest of the gang climb up onto the caisson and queue at the first of the air locks. The steel bolts and gauges make it look like a submarine or industrial boiler. The shaft is narrow, not much wider than their shoulders. They leave ten seconds between each man to avoid panic. They're sinkers, working in compressed air to dig Pier 6 of the new bridge into the harbour bed. From the rig they can see Auckland Harbour thrumming: ferries on the water, cars on the waterfront, trucks and diggers beetling around the viaducts on the approach roads north and south.

Last night at the Albion was their final briefing. Jim sipped modestly but routinely. He let his cigarettes slow him down and avoided putting his elbow in the puddle of beer on the leaner between them. Chopper was the youngest of them. He was known for his skills as an axeman, so he informed them all—jigger chop champion at the Wanganui A&P. When he wasn't talking about himself or necking his beer, which wasn't very often, Chopper listened with the others while the foreman described some of the effects of working in thirty pounds of air pressure. Considering how much beer the kid had put away, it was hardly surprising that he would need to go to the toilet. With an entire gang to brief, it's hardly surprising that the foreman would continue without him. We can assume that when they line up to go down, Chopper has missed out on one piece of information in particular, and the rest of the gang know he has. He is last in line.

In the air-shaft, the foreman sets the tone at silent, so all they hear is the soft slaps of their own hands landing and the louder ringing out of boots hitting the rungs. Eight different sets of boots find their mark in alternating rhythms, the reverberations overlapping to create a hum. They can see their arms and hands in the light from their headlamps and, if they point their heads down, their feet. Their animal instincts tell them they're going in the wrong bloody direction. The foreman is down into the working chamber first. He lights the fixed lamps. Each man turns his own headlamp off when he clears the ladder. A few remove their helmets and take in their new environment—the air pocket of curved steel, tinny sounds. The first bucket, a discordant bell, collides with the sides of the muck shaft on its way down. To a man they loiter there, waiting. Jim lights a cigarette but it burns down too fast. His life is being used up more quickly down here.

After the second-to-last man has reached the bottom, one of them steps forward and rubs something on the last rung of the ladder. Chopper increases his pace to catch up.

His legs arrive first, then his boot hits the bottom rung and goes out from under him. He lands squarely on his backpack in the mud. 'Shit, what the bloody—' His voice comes out like Donald Duck, as though he's been inhaling helium. The expression on his face, priceless already, gets even better.

Katherine

Her glasses slid off her nose and she pushed them up again. Their guide poled them along, a grown Tom Sawyer in a ranger's uniform and wide-brimmed hat. He whistled a birdcall. 'Look here, three o'clock.' Ninety degrees from the bow was a kingbird, elegant in black and white. 'Six, behind you.' Turtles, one large and two tiny, plopping into the water off the tangled mess of a dead tree trunk. They glided through a cypress forest that was submerged to its knees and trailing rags of Spanish moss, sky a distant blue mist. Katherine could only apply perhaps half of her usual level of concentration; the rest was taken up in wonder at the heat.

From time to time a fisherman would wave towards Katherine's group from a ramshackle fishing throne on the bank. 'Damn.' A cormorant had lifted off from the top branch of a water oak before Roy, Marcia's husband, could take its photograph.

'The huntin' and fishin' preserve is maintained by a constant depth of water,' the guide said.

Katherine watched a spider pick its way from leaf to leaf of the waterweed beside the boat. If she were at home she would drag her hand in and let the water bulge and slip around it, but not here. There were houseboats back in amongst the thickets—tree houses suspended by water.

They saw egrets, bald eagles and a night heron jerking a fish down its gullet, the slick tail flapping in its beak. Katherine lined up a cluster of woodpecker chicks in the viewfinder of her camera, their necks waving from their hole high up in a tree trunk. 'Ladies, I'm going to ask you to turn this way, twelve to six is your range, please.' Her camera's viewing window was small and it took all of her attention to keep the chicks in sight. She was stretching the range of the lens she had fitted. She cocked the shutter, depressed the button, and only then raised her head. Roy whistled.

'Someone got 'im.' It was hardly more than a whisper.

'Where are we looking?' she asked. The range from twelve to six was where the trees thinned out and gave way to lake, and was devoid of creatures, as far as she could tell. The heat was especially fierce deep into the trees where they were, sheltered from any breeze. Marcia had fixed her gaze out at the lake, on nothing in particular Katherine could make out. An iridescent dragonfly had landed on her skirt, perhaps attracted by the print, a riot of raspberries.

'What he's doing here I don't know,' the guide said. The two men's drawls were subtly distinct, the guide's Cajun vowels disorientating, but, more than that, she could tell they were facing the other direction. She turned into the evening range of the clock face for long enough to see a flat-bottomed barge loaded with racks of moss, then, on an impulse, she turned back. 'Prob'ly someone saw him throwing his fish scraps in. They'll get the gators comin' round, takin' a baby.' Their boat slid through water that was still as a vast puddle, tree roots spreading to grip the soil beneath. A high peeping carried to them from a warbler.

'Speaking of which,' the guide said. 'Ten o'clock.' A dark head with a snout as long as a dinner platter slid through the surface no more than a few feet away. Its eyes were hooded, and dragon spikes protruded on what might be considered the back of its neck.

'Oh, there one is,' Marcia said. The alligator dipped out of sight as though it had heard her.

'What are your natural predators in your country?' the guide asked. Katherine didn't realise he was addressing her at first.

'None, not that threaten people,' she said, 'because we're so isolated.'

She removed her damp hand from Roy's, which was smooth and cool, as soon as her feet found the wharf. Marcia's fan beat the air in her peripheral vision. 'Can we drive you anywhere on our way back?' she asked. The guide pushed off again and started his motor. 'Roy, how about the camp? She might like to see that.' A fuzzy-headed boy brought a box of lemonade down to greet them with. 'Quarter a pop' was scrawled on the side. When they shook their heads no thanks, he blinked and wheeled his trolley off again, presumably to put the box back in a chiller somewhere. Their tour was the last of the day.

'They don't have houseboats in New Zealand?'

'Not like yours,' Katherine said.

Roy studied his shoes. Drinks hour was approaching. 'We'll take you down there,' he said. 'But be warned, they're likely to ask you on board and force-feed you their boudin.'

'I couldn't eat a thing at the moment,' she said.

'You tell them, see how far it gets you.'

The dirt road widened out in a swampside dead end where a row of houseboats was moored and two trucks parked up. This was the working side of the boats, hung with nets, grappling hooks and washing coppers. 'Some people live on these, some people live in town and come out,' Roy said. He shut off the engine, opened the driver's door and got out. When Katherine opened her door a scrawny dog skittered off on a diagonal. Roy leaned an elbow on the car's roof. 'They'll still speak French, but not to the extent they did.' At the back of one of the boats a woman was hanging clothes over a line.

'There's a hummingbird,' Marcia said. 'On that jasmine over there.' She knew Katherine liked them. Katherine lifted her binoculars towards the corner of a collapsing boatshed, but as usual the bird veered around far too much and far too fast for her to focus on it. She did see something else moving, further out in the water, to one side of the shed. She saw their guide on the moss-collecting barge they had passed. He was bent forward, lifting a Negro man from his shoulders. She almost blurted out a shocked reaction, then she didn't.

'What have you got there?' Roy asked. 'No hummingbird's staying that still.'

On the water, in the rounds of her binoculars, the guide shuffled forward until the man was lying parallel to the tour boat. He stepped down, lifted him under his shoulders and dragged him in. The man's legs dropped heavily. 'Our guide, helping a man who's hurt.'

'Someone hurt out there?' Marcia asked. The guide was untying the boat, starting the motor.

'Who's that now?' Roy asked.

'They're coming in,' Katherine said. She lowered the binoculars. 'He took him into his boat,' she said. 'A Negro.' The flat blat of the boat's motor was growing louder, and she could see where the prow would nose in amongst the weeds. The woman at the back of her boat had left her clothesline and was peering around the corner.

Roy opened the car door wide and sat back in the driver's seat. 'They'll see he gets the help he needs.'

'Do you think these old trucks will run?' Katherine asked. One of them didn't have a bonnet and its motor was exposed to the open air.

'They'll look after him,' Roy said.

Marcia sat back in her seat and closed the door.

'Thirty seconds—I'll just take a photograph,' Katherine said, as Roy closed his door too. She walked halfway to the houseboat. 'Excuse me,' she said. People would later interpret the woman's expression as hostile, but Katherine knew she was just surprised.

Jim

The meeting room was oversized for the fifteen or so men who were in it. It had an aroma of underuse, and was hung with patients' artwork. One watercolour must have depicted Men's Bay originally but the bluff in the foreground had been painted over in muddy colours until it commanded the frame. 'Father give us the courage to change what must be altered, serenity to accept what cannot be helped, and the insight to know one from the other.' They chanted it in unison.

Captain Mac started. 'My name is Bob and I'm an alcoholic.'

'Hi Bob.'

The captain was still stocky, Jim thought, had obviously been pugnacious once upon a time, but he'd been domesticated. Not by his wife, or not only by her—by the big man in the clouds.

'I want to start today by welcoming Jim.'

'Hi Jim.' They chanted it together.

'Jim got here in September. He's from down south originally.' Nods here and there.

'Whereabouts, Jim?'

'Invercargill.'

'Doesn't get much further south than that.'

'Not much.'

'You're very welcome,' Captain Mac went on. 'We normally have some notices to start things off. I've got to let you know that next week's meeting will be held in the library. There'll be displays in here of crafts and bits and pieces. We've got Miss Morton coming of course, then we'll leave it here for the visiting committee. Lastly, we're planning a trip from the Auckland City chapter in April. Early days yet but I'll get back to you with more details. We'll put something on, make a night of it.'

'Couple of kegs?'

Captain Mac didn't miss a beat. 'At the very least.'

The universe couldn't tolerate a man having more than his share of fun, was all. You either eked it out over a lifetime or you gorged. Jim had once seen his son, when he was given a sixpenny mixture, take one lolly out to eat at a time then roll the paper bag closed again. Jim would never have done that.

'Everyone comes to AA in a different way,' the captain said. 'I thought I'd tell you tonight about one member of the fellowship, another Jim, who took himself to the house of a good friend of mine, sat on the porch and started reciting a poem to their dog.' This raised a few laughs. 'The poem was called "Hound of Heaven". It starts, "I fled Him down the nights and down the days." A few lines on it says, "In the

69

midst of tears I hid from Him, and under running laughter.'"

In the embarrassed pause, the captain looked up from the page he was holding. Always this feeling when there were God-botherers about, as though someone was lifting at the edges of your brain. They'd take the top off if they could.

'That's good, isn't it?' the captain said. 'The man who wrote it had his own problems. So Jim chose this poem, all 182 lines of it, to do his talking for him. None of the rest of us could remember so much, but the point is, he found his way. That first step is probably the hardest, isn't it? To admit that you're powerless?' The Captain lowered his head again. '"I hid from Him", it says. These footsteps follow him throughout the whole poem, "with unhurrying chase, And unperturbèd pace". He's talking about God of course, but it also applies to the truth, doesn't it? You can't shake it. You have to stop and turn around.'

Back on the mainland, Jim thought, he'd get a few months on the girders with a hammer somewhere and look for the next thing. He'd chat up the girl in the TAB.

'Who would like to speak next? Thank you Frank.'

'My name's Frank and I'm an alcoholic.' Frank looked as though he'd been punched in the stomach years ago and never straightened up.

'Hi Frank.'

'The first time I was incarcerated for my drinking was early on, as a young man, and I was in and out of trouble for a long time.' He was one of the old-timers, seventy at least. 'My rock bottom was probably in prison but I carried on getting drunk when I got out. I remembered the other day one of the best jobs I ever had, as a cook for a logging gang. I kept that fire going all day and too right did I know I was appreciated.

They got rid of me when I burnt the bread once too often, so I camped out for the summer instead. When my boots were knackered I didn't want to shell out for new ones, the whisky was more important, so I went without, got feet like a Maori.'

Captain Mac was staring down at his black clodhopper lace-ups, listening. He must have heard it all before but he listened anyway.

'When I came to the island,' Frank said. 'I lost the desire to drink. Not at the start, not even the first time, but after I stuck at it. You men are lucky. Until recently there were no meetings, no one-on-ones, no picnics.'

'Thank you Frank.'

'There was one manager carried a gun.'

'Who's next? Thanks Hemi.'

'My name's Hemi and I'm an alcoholic.'

'Hi Hemi.'

'I've been here two weeks, and it's two weeks since I had a drink.'

'Do you want to tell us what happened two weeks ago?' Captain Mac asked.

'My mates stitched me up. That's what I think anyway.' Hemi was big, not just broad but tall as well. Something about the moody curve of his lips made Jim uneasy, so he looked out the window behind him at the lights from the hospital block instead. 'This fulla Skek was saying things about my missus, how I should treat her, then out of nowhere he starts giving me brandy and says he'll loan me a pound to go out. We head down to the pub, all okay, then this Panguru Maori comes over and says keep it down. His uncle can't hear or something. He looked at me like I was scum. So I waited until closing and put the boot in. Cop saw me.'

'How's life been going since your last stretch?'

'Going well. I was with the Power Board. Then my daughter got sick. Anyway, I do want to straighten myself up. I'd rather be here than in jail.'

'Thank you Hemi,' Captain Mac said. If boots were being put in, Hemi would be one to stay clear of. 'Gerald.'

Gerald told them he was working on the eighth step. 'Good on you, Gerald,' Captain Mac said. 'Number eight, for anyone who doesn't know, is about making a list of people you've harmed. The steps are up on the wall there.'

'It's hard,' Gerald said. 'Hard to think of all the things you've done.' Some of this AA was about feeling sorry for yourself, Jim was beginning to realise. Gerald was shaking his balding head, wallowing in it. 'This one memory has been bothering me, a lass who got up the courage to come to a meeting. Not a word of a lie: there she was, telling her story to all these men, head down, trying not to cry, the whole bit, and my heart just went out to her, you know? I asked her to have a cup of tea with me afterwards. Swear to God, I just wanted to help her at the start.' He exhaled and shook his head. 'Well, while she was talking to me in this tearooms she began to relax a bit. She wasn't old, around late twenties, nice face when she cheered up. Her cheeks were all rosy, you know. She was right there.'

Gerald held a hand up, palm open. He wasn't handsome but sometimes they weren't; if they found the right one (or the wrong one), they could push the buttons and she'd light up like Christmas.

'Anyway, she was drinking again the last I heard. I stopped going to those meetings.'

Lorna

She gave Isaac his bottle while they listened to an interview with an actor who had starred in a film. Going by the metallic rattle in the kitchen and the smell, scones were on their way. Her feet basked in a sunny square of carpet. 'Where's London?' she asked him. 'What's there?' His slack little arms and bowed baby legs had got fatter. One of his arms flailed out sideways. With the hand that wasn't holding the bottle she tried to smooth his hair down. Each time she smoothed, it bounced back, though eventually less. After a while his suckling slowed down, then stopped altogether. When he was content like that, so was she, but the peace never lasted long. That was her mum beside her, and those were her mum's arms reaching down to lift him away.

'I've got the cot ready,' her mum whispered. 'Why don't you go for a walk, get some fresh air.'

'You always take him off me,' Lorna complained.

'He shouldn't be held all the time.'

'You're holding him!'

Her mum began swaying back and forth. 'I want him to sleep.'

'He was going to sleep.'

'You've been stewing in your own juices long enough. It's easier to cuddle a baby than it is to get on with your own things.'

'He is my own thing.'

Her mum looked at the ceiling as though to seek help from above. 'Hadn't you better get a job?'

Isaac watched them, alert to something in their tone. He often rejected Lorna's efforts to soothe him, but no matter how ugly he got, Lorna was up and moving whenever he cried, before she'd even had a chance to think about it. His face had filled out and got round. He didn't look permanently worried anymore. Instead he went straight from curious to upset, an angry moon boy.

Lorna could have said more, could have said Isaac was all she had left, but that would only have spurred her mum on, so she did as she was told and set out along the driveway towards the road in the open air, in the quiet. They weren't in a neighbourhood now. There weren't any adults gardening or gates creaking, just a hiss of breeze in the poplars. Their driveway was a flash past in a stranger's journey. Nearer the road, she picked and held out a palmful of grass for next door's bay mare, which had made its way over to the corner fence. The horse rubbered the blades in with her mobile lips. Beyond the mare's paddock, a car crept along the road towards them. Lorna couldn't see anyone driving until it got closer and she spied an older woman clutching the steering wheel. The driver didn't have to reduce her speed by much to pull over onto the verge.

The window was open on the passenger side and the foot-well was stuffed with carry bags, they themselves stuffed with magazines. The driver was wearing trousers, not a skirt. 'Do you live here?' she asked.

'Down this drive,' Lorna said.

The woman nodded. 'The Sayers' old place. We knew the Sayers. We're up on the heights.' She pointed to the slopes that dipped to meet the road further along. 'On an orchard.' She was wrinkled, but not slumped or watery-eyed like most old ladies. 'Do you catch the school bus?'

'I don't go to school,' Lorna said.

'What do you do?'

'I've been sick.'

'You don't look sick. Are you in the Country Girls?'

'No.'

'Where do you go to church?'

'I don't know yet.'

She looked at Lorna—not just looked, but studied her eyes. 'What do you do, by yourself all the time?'

Lorna didn't answer her. It was easy to fail the normality test. Everyone treated them differently, people they ran into on the street or in shops; people soon gave up on conversations. 'Isn't it exciting about the Harbour Bridge?' they'd say. 'Thanks be to God,' her mum would say, as though everybody needed to be reminded, all the time. You were normal if your father went to hotels and your mother sat on committees.

'Well.' The old woman gave up and concentrated on

working the gearbox instead. 'Better get on.' She waved, and the car rumbled away.

Lorna's parents had left the Church of Jesus Christ, even though the prophet David McKay had visited from America and announced that a temple was going to be built in the Waikato. A *temple*. Lorna's dad might have become a labour missionary. She might have attended the school and had a temple marriage.

She eased the latch on the door when she got back, but Isaac was still awake. 'Lorna, look.' Her mum was on the settee, holding him up under his arms. Isaac was clueless, had no idea his cheeks were so pudgy or his hair was sticking up again. He gazed at Lorna's mum as she blew through her lips to make them vibrate. 'Phrrrr.' His wide, staring eyes relaxed. She did it again, and the corners of his mouth pulled his lips open. 'Who's a silly baby?' her mum said. 'Who's a silly baby with silly hair?' Isaac's smile remained for a moment longer, then just seemed to pass, like weather. Finally he noticed Lorna, and went back to his usual goggle-eyed stare.

'I didn't know he could smile,' she said. It came out as an accusation. The undercurrents were always there. She always got caught in them.

'He'll be smiling at everything soon enough. He'll smile when he fills his nappy.' Her mum began to twist around then thought better of it. 'Come around here so I can talk to you.' She sat Isaac on her knee. She'd said less about her back recently, but that didn't mean it was better, necessarily. She might just have more to distract her. 'Where did you go for your walk?'

'To the end of the drive. An old lady stopped in her car and asked me if I was in the Country Girls.'

'Did she?' Her mum looked down towards Isaac's feet. 'What else did she ask you?'

'She asked me about church. I didn't tell her I got kicked out of the last one.'

'That's enough.'

Lorna was 'Lolo' and her mum was 'Mama' when Isaac began to say words. He'd inherited her mum's curly hair but his chunky arms and legs were a surprise, and so were the tantrums he began to have once he was standing and cruising from one piece of furniture to another, tantrums during which he'd collapse in a heap, as though whatever they'd done wrong had chased his spirit from his body. He'd stay on the floor for who knew how long; not even he knew, he'd have to turn his head and peek up at them eventually. Sometimes Lorna could tickle him out of it, sometimes he'd yell to express even deeper offence. On certain days, when her mum hadn't baked, while the world went on without her and there was nothing to distract her from the bleakness of home, she imagined he was punishing her.

★

Lorna's mum sat down to wait for the bus one day at her usual stop in front of the library. She placed her shopping bag at her feet, with its purchases from the chemist, McFarlane's Fabrics and the butcher's (sausages for tea, with a saveloy for Isaac). She noticed a crowd gathered around the front window at Farmers across the road, where three men in shorts and Hawaiian shirts were playing ukuleles, or were they banjos? Their song must have finished, and they left the window to make way for a woman holding a little girl who was dressed up like a doll in a brand new summer outfit. Lorna's mum couldn't see the details of what the tot was wearing, her sandals or the print on her dress, but the dear wee puffball was all skirts, she told Lorna and her dad afterwards, more fabric than child. While she was watching, the bus had approached. She still had time to get ready, to collect herself and unzip her purse, people always got off there for the shops, but she panicked and went for her handbag in a hurry, and the sudden movement disturbed a cranky nerve in her lower back.

She had to sit leaning forward with her elbows on knees, as though she'd tired herself out shopping and didn't have the gumption to sit up. Now I've done it, she thought. Lorna was at home with Isaac and wouldn't know where she'd got to. She shook her head at the bus driver to send him on, rather than have to lift her arm. She stared at the kerb, waiting for her mind to wake up and tell her what to do. This was the state she was in when two people stopped in front of her, or more precisely two pairs of sensible black lace-ups, the bottom of a pair of black trouser legs, and black nylons and the hem of a black skirt.

'Are you all right?' It was the woman who'd asked, and Lorna's mum raised her head a little higher, high enough to see the bottom of two jackets and gather than they must be wearing uniforms. They might be parking wardens. The woman held a stack of printed cards in one hand.

'I've hurt my back,' said Lorna's mum.

The woman dropped into a crouch: epaulettes, a high collar with a metal-stamped S and a bonnet. They were Sallies. 'You're stuck here, are you?'

What more could a person expect from the Lord, Lorna's mum would ask them later, than to be rescued by two of His representatives, two soldiers, in a time of need? How many young people dedicated their lives to serving others? The female officer had sat with Lorna's mum while the man went to their church just a few doors down to use the telephone. Eventually the pain had eased off enough for her to sit up and conceive of standing. She asked the woman for one of the cards she was holding. Printed on it was Psalm 118:24: *This is the day which Jehovah hath made; We will rejoice and be glad in it.* Later on in that day Jehovah had made, after Lorna's dad, still in his overalls, had changed Isaac's nappy, and while they were eating the lumpy gravy Lorna had made to go with the sausages, her mum told them that the officers' appearance had been no coincidence. Their family had sought God out, she said, but they had chosen the wrong door, and now He was gathering them back in.

They attended their first service in a citadel that wasn't quite a church but wasn't a hall either. Lorna was less able to let her mind wander than she had during the meetings of the Latter-day Saints, because there was more going on, so much noise and activity. A brass band played music. A timbrel brigade got up and did a routine, four girls in blouses with epaulettes, either celebrating the gospel or just showing off. Then the children filed out when it was time for the sermon, trying so hard to be good it made their movements jerky. The officer who gave the sermon talked about a Bible verse for ages; there was nothing new in that, but he was more impassioned than the branch president had been, more like a band-leader than a businessman. When it came to the blessings, he moved down the aisle to stand beside a girl who had polio. She was strapped into a leg brace with her crutches propped up beside her.

'Prayers of thanks to the scientists in America,' he said, 'who are developing a vaccine for this savage disease.' He lifted his arms to hover nearer the girl. 'And prayers of strength for this family.' The girl bowed her head, either praying or avoiding everyone's gaze. 'God help us to trust and to battle for good; it is not for us to know your will.'

In a back room afterwards, holding an oddly bulging scone that was unfit for sale at the local bakery, Lorna looked around at the clean faces and brushed hair, the men with their shirts tucked in and sleeves rolled down, and she got the feeling most of them didn't quite fit in elsewhere. They were like the scones. God must at least appreciate the effort they took to present themselves every Sunday morning, even if it was the bare minimum He could expect.

Her mum introduced her to Lieutenant Eng, the young woman who had helped at the bus stop. The lieutenant had the palest blond hair Lorna had ever seen. Her eyebrows were almost invisible. She stroked the back of Isaac's hand. 'Your mother told me about you,' she said, 'both of you.' Not everything, she didn't, Lorna thought, but she knew the lieutenant was trying to be nice. She hadn't mentioned the age gap between Lorna and Isaac. When people did, Lorna's mum called him 'our little surprise'.

'We have lots of groups in the corps looking for members,' Lieutenant Eng said. 'The songsters, the timbrel brigade and the youth corps.'

Lorna's mum squeezed her hand.

'The timbrels were good,' Lorna said. All the glory, without much experience required, that was how it had seemed to her.

Her dad interrupted them. He was standing to attention again because he'd brought someone over. 'Mr Purcell manages the local sawmill,' he said. Mr Purcell was hollow-cheeked, as though the air had been sucked out of him. He nodded around to them while her dad spoke, caught up in a loop of greeting and agreement.

'They need someone in the office to file and type,' Lorna's dad said, 'so I told him I knew just the girl.'

★

The whining of the saws carried down the bank to the office where only Mr Purcell and Lorna were permanently installed, though the foreman was in and out, and the sawyers with their dusty hair. Whenever they had smoko in the yard they were relaxed, pies or cigarettes in hand, but in the office before the typewriter and filing cabinets they were more polite and laughed less. Lorna learned the difference between dry and green weight, between dressed and undressed. She learned what could go wrong, about holes and gum streak, about growth stress. She envied them the fragrance they worked in hour after hour and day after day, and the way the sun, with the great doors open, slanted in and blessed their efforts, as they brought the forest indoors.

The drivers of the front-end loaders always called in at the office after they rumbled into the yard. Among them was Alan, who would talk about films he'd seen at the weekend. Something with one of the Jameses, Dean or Stewart, or Marilyn Monroe. *Forbidden Planet*. He was English, from 'the North'. It was different up there, he told Lorna, none of the guards in furry hats or la-de-dah. He swaggered in through the door one morning and stopped. Mr Purcell looked up from his desk and Lorna from her typewriter. 'How goes it Alan?' Mr Purcell asked.

'No prison can hold me,' Alan used a slow American drawl. 'No army defeat me.' He loitered in the doorway. '*The Conqueror*,' he said in his normal voice. 'You should go Lorna. It were right good.' Lorna had seen the poster for the film—it was the kind with a woman in a scanty dress. 'Tell you what else you should've seen: my nephew, last night,' Alan said. He shook his head. His hair was cut short at the sides but left long on top. 'Picks up my father's pipe and sticks his fingers into it. Soot everywhere—all over his fingers, his face. Looks at us, not a clue.'

'My brother chased a duck into the creek last week and fell in after it,' Lorna said.

Alan gave an exaggerated start. She didn't often speak up. 'Were he drunk?' he asked.

Mr Purcell held out his hand to Alan. 'Come on, let's have your docket then.'

That weekend Lorna wiped condensation off the bus window with a glove and looked for familiar landmarks in the smeared view. Greer's orchards and the trotting track, the wrecker's yard and the Wayside Inn on the corner, and eventually footpaths and traffic lights, blobs of colour through the gloom. Isaac would have enjoyed the ride, she thought, would have been impressed by the strangers all seated facing forwards. The boy in the booth at the Kiwi didn't seem surprised that she was there alone, only handed over her ticket for the matinee and smiled routinely. Faces shifted and surged around her in the foyer, including a girl from her high school with a boyfriend or fiancé, but Lorna was allowed to be there, tucking her ticket into her pocket and spending her change on a choc-dip. One child stared at her, but only because he wanted to beg his mother for an ice cream. '*Please*.' She was allowed to climb the carpeted stairs, follow the usherette's torch and sidestep down a row to an empty seat, sink down into murmurs and silhouettes, and nobody need say anything about it.

She stood and let her seat flip up with everyone else's when the first few bars of the anthem came in. Then they watched a Popeye cartoon, met his giant friend, saw them compete for Olive's attention, Olive in a red blouse in her city apartment, Popeye flexing his tattooed biceps. In the Pictorial Parade, soldiers jumped their motorcycles in a display for the Queen of Tonga. After the adverts the screen went blank. Lorna took a bite of her ice cream and some pieces of chocolate shell fell off. She heard, 'Ladies and gentlemen, a special musical presentation before your feature . . .' She couldn't see much in the dimness. The best she could do was pat her blouse in the area where the chocolate had fallen. 'Rock Around the Clock!'

A lone voice whooped in the darkness. A man on the screen with a round face and a curl on his forehead counted around the clock, then the beat came in. The music didn't seem to come from the band, they seemed to have used their instruments to tap into a stream that was flowing already. Lorna sensed a subtle jump of muscles from several people nearby. Girls in the row in front of her bounced their knees in time. Heads dipped. A saxophone burst in. For the length of the song, it was as though an electrical current had been sent through all of the seats, and when it stopped the switch was flicked off. The audience on the recording applauded. Children had to be settled. The opening credits of *Lady and the Tramp* rolled away and the film began while a piece of chocolate melted unnoticed on Lorna's chest.

———

'One two three o'clock . . .' She sang quietly to herself while squeezing the toothpaste on. The Thursday night hit parade. The rich pause and crackle of dust when the needle was placed on a record. Get ready, it said. Something was about to start. The crooners were kissing at the start of their songs and married by the end. 'Will we have rainbows?' Doris Day sang in 'Que Sera, Sera'. No one got married in rock and roll. Side tap, side tap, back-forward. Dancing to Cotton-Eyed Joe's 'Big Beat Ball' with her door closed. Stopping for Elvis Presley's voice, sobby and unwholesome, in 'Heartbreak Hotel'.

She took the bus to Takapuna again, this time to Milne and Choyce, where she'd never been before. She had to force herself to walk past the doorman, past racks of Max Factor and Lanvin (a girl and her mother bent over a cabinet, the same round to their shoulders, the same slim noses), through millinery, past tiers of rotating feet in all shades cut off below the knee, all the way to the lift. She didn't fit in, but she persevered because the newspaper had said the records counter at Millins was excellent: 'a superb selection for your listening delectation'.

The record bins were in front of her, beyond a row of chairs and coffee tables, when the lift doors opened. She had got as far as lifting a cover out and flipping it over when he approached her. He wasn't in uniform but she recognised him from somewhere, the dark glasses especially. They made him mysterious. He couldn't be blind, not without a stick. 'I think I've seen you at church,' he said. 'With your family. I'm Paul Hendry.'

Later, when she knew him better, Paul told her that he wouldn't normally have approached someone in his civilian clothes, that he had spoken to her because she was from his church and, when she pressed him, perhaps because she had seemed a bit lost (Johnny Devlin: he had seen the record before she'd pushed it back into the bin). She never told him, not even after they became friends, that the uniform would have put her off.

'Is Birkenhead your church?' she asked.

'It's my uncle's church, but we're actually here on a campaign. I'm in officer training at the college in Wellington.' She remembered the campaigners then, the 'Intercessors', from their service the Sunday before. They had spoken about an after-school rally they'd held, and their door-to-door bombardments. So he was an odd scone too.

Paul smiled, showing dimples. 'Don't tell anyone you saw me here in mufti.' She couldn't see his eyes to know whether he was sincere.

No one was paying them any attention. In the next department a saleswoman was positioning shoes. Back the other way an overweight man was clicking the cords of lamps; a few lit up, not all. The melody coming over the speakers was turned down low, as though they were in a fish tank.

'I'm looking at brass band music,' he said. 'Probably a bit predictable. What do you like?'

'I'm just browsing,' Lorna said. It was awkward, yet he remained.

'Do you normally go shopping by yourself?' he asked.

'It's my day off too,' she said, 'from work,' not in answer to his question but trying to seem less of a delinquent, in case that was what he thought she was. 'I work at Burton's Sawmill.'

'I know the manager there,' Paul said. He was already scanning his knowledge of the mill for anything relevant. Lorna could tell, despite not being able to see his eyes.

'Mr Purcell?'

'That's him, he's friends with my uncle.'

She herself had thought of something, not connected, but worth mentioning. 'Did you know the owner is called Mr Pine?'

'Mr Pine? No.' This time the dimples stayed for a while. He wasn't a heartthrob, but something about him, the combination of sunglasses and dimples, prevented Lorna from making an excuse to leave. 'I had a music teacher called Gordon Strummer,' he said.

'What did he play?'

'Piano, mainly.'

'Can I help you with anything?' The shop assistant had come out from behind the counter.

'No thanks, we're just browsing,' Paul said. The salesman looked at each of them one more time and retreated. Lorna would have been scared away, if she'd been alone.

'Sorry, what's your name?' Paul asked.

'Oh, it's Lorna,' she said.

'Nice to meet you.' His arms floated out from his sides, and his hands slapped the sides of his legs gently. 'Listen, I don't know how much involvement you have with the corps,' he said, 'but a couple of us are going to be making tea at a dance on Saturday, if you want to help.'

'At the Coronation Hall?' she asked.

'At the Pirate Shippe, in Milford.'

He might be trying to recruit her for the cause, but she did want to find out what kind of music they'd play. His sunglasses didn't tell her much. 'Okay,' she said. 'I'll help.'

———

The lounge smelt of burning coal and chops hissing in the oven when Paul called around with his comrade Bill to collect Lorna. Her dad shook both of their hands. Bill had a prominent chest and his ears sprang out sideways when he took his hat off. Paul was only a few inches taller than Lorna, but he was all in proportion. A breeze was cutting through the warmth of the fire from the kitchen window. Lorna's dad would tell her mum to close it soon, to keep the heat in.

'You bumped into each other in Takapuna, is that right?' her mum asked. The combination of the steam and the stirring of the breeze had frizzed out her hair and the front pocket of her apron bulged with a handkerchief or half-darned sock she'd stuffed in. Lorna's dad had cried out the previous night, for the first time in ages.

'We got talking at the record counter at Milne and Choyce,' Paul said.

'Milne and Choyce,' her mum said. 'Did you?'

'Can we shut that window?' Her dad was in his armchair, in his slippers. 'Sit down for a minute, you two.'

'Out!' Isaac yelled from his highchair in the kitchen. He was getting too big for it. Lorna's mum brought him in.

'This is Lorna's brother Isaac,' her dad said. Isaac stared at Paul, then at Bill. What might happen next, if two strangers could walk through the door? 'Are you in a band, Paul?' her dad asked.

'That I am, on cornet,' Paul said. 'Bill plays a trombone.'

'So you're both doing your officer training?'

'Just wonderful, the dedication of you young people,' her mum said.

'Tombo,' Isaac said. A few days ago Lorna hadn't known

Paul, and now he was sitting in her mum's chair, still wearing his glasses, though no one commented on those.

They weren't inside the Olde Pirate Shippe as Lorna had expected, but in a tea van, looking out over the waves. Leaning from the serving window she could just see the prow, with its rows of porthole windows and mast. In the fading sunlight, Bill secured the awning while Lorna set out cups and saucers and Paul fitted the gas bottle. Couples and groups stepped over drifts of sand under the electric lanterns, girls in home-sewn dresses, boys in clean shirts, with and without slicked up hair. Paul greeted two young men on their way past, one tall and one shorter. 'Cup of tea?' he asked.

'Is it true that you have to wash people's feet?' the taller one said.

'We try to follow Jesus's example,' Bill said. The tall man loped over and Lorna poured a cup—she had to use both hands to lift the teapot—and added milk.

The tall man took small sips of his tea, one after the other. 'Did Jesus have a tea van?'

'He probably would've,' Paul said. 'If he thought it would help people.' The smaller man smirked up at his taller friend, who took a few final sips and put his cup down.

'Nice sunglasses,' he said.

'All that goo they put in their hair,' Paul said when they were out of earshot. 'Melts in the heat and drips down their faces.' It was the first time she'd heard him sound anything but good-natured.

The next person to stop was further along in years. He shuffled towards them with his jacket hanging open. He'd missed loops in belting his trousers. At the counter he pulled himself up straight and snapped a hand to his forehead in a sudden salute. 'May I please have a cup of your finest tea?' he asked. His stance wasn't steady and nor was his gaze. Bill put a hand on Lorna's arm when she had only half filled the cup.

'That'll do,' he said. She put the cup down on the counter. Now she was catching hints of a complex odour.

'Tide's gone out, hasn't it?' The man looked at her chest. 'I like your badge.' They watched him sway ever so slowly back and forth. He'd come close to spilling his drink, then start back the other way. 'Not dancing tonight?' he asked.

'Too busy out here,' Lorna said.

'Where are you living?' Paul asked him.

'I'm staying with my daughter. She's back in there.' He indicated with his head the neighbourhood behind them, across the road. 'Better go. See you on the poop deck.'

'Cup please,' Paul said. The man returned his cup to the counter as gently as he could, gave them a last salute and moved off away from the Shippe's lights.

'A hot drink and a friendly face,' Bill said. 'That's all you can do sometimes.'

Inside the Old Pirate Shippe a woman at a desk with a tin box, stamp and inkpad called Lorna dear and waved her through the foyer, through the pulse of amplified music. Lorna hadn't counted on the jostle in the toilets or the bosom buddies and brash gossip, so she pushed open the door and got out as soon as she could. Someone stopped her on her way back through the foyer.

'Eh up, it's Lorna.' It was Alan from the mill, strange in a roomy jacket and tapered trousers. 'Who are you here with?'

She pointed to her badge. 'I'm in the tea van outside.'

'I didn't know you were of the Sallies persuasion.

Have you been in?' The doors beside them opened into a ballroom, cavernous and populated, but a wall of backs blocked Lorna's view.

'I'm not dressed for it.'

'Never mind that. You'll come in for a peek, won't you?'

On the dance floor, the waltzing girls were composed, different creatures than in the toilets. Dusty memorabilia hung from the walls: lanterns on chains, antique swords. 'Let's go upstairs first.' Alan led her along the back wall, up the staircase to another dance floor. They walked to the far end, towards the view of the water and Rangitoto, past couples huddled up on benches. 'Look at this,' he said, and he pointed behind the benches to a line of hatches that let the sound through from downstairs. Lorna leaned over and peered through the grille nearest to her, down at the double bass player, who stood waiting with his arms resting around his instrument's neck.

'Hope you're all enjoying yourselves,' she heard. 'We're going to liven things up for you now.' With that, the couples were up from the benches in a flurry and headed for the stairs. Lorna and Alan followed, not quite running but carried along. When they got to the bottom and stopped, people flowed around them onto the floor. The traffic wasn't all one way, there were couples walking off the floor as well. '*Well it's one for the money*'—crunch of guitar and drums—'*two for the show.*' They came in again, stopped. '*Three to get ready, now go cat go.*' Lorna froze up with excitement, forgot her patched cardigan and lace-ups.

'Come on,' Alan said.

'I can't.'

'You'll be fine.' He held his hand out. 'You were already

moving, in case you hadn't noticed. Just bring it out here.'

She wasn't drawn in close to him, which was a relief, and he stuck with the simple side-to-side, so before long she could check around to see that most couples were doing the same. Alan leaned in. 'Look at you go!'

'You can burn my house, steal my car, drink my liquor from an old fruit jar.'

'Eh up, look,' he said. A few couples were doing lifts after all. They stopped to watch, clapping the beat. One of the girls slid through her partner's legs onto the floor and he whipped around to pull her up. The band repeated the refrain, then again. Two arms flung wide caught Lorna's attention—two dancers nearby, their limbs stretched open like the points of two stars: the moment when a young man yanked his partner in.

There was something about the direction he pulled from, and his angle when he leaned forward to roll her. She made contact in the wrong position and landed awkwardly across him, rag-doll-like, and hard. Her necklace bounced off her chest. Her partner straightened up to see what had happened and she slid sideways, unresisting, to land on the floor beside him.

Everyone who had seen it stood stock still. The drumbeat stopped, the last few bars and lyrics died away and the girl's partner waved an arm above his head. He crouched down beside her. At first, the other dancers all gaped, as though she had dropped out of the sky. She had been in the toilets when Lorna was there, applying the coral lipstick she was wearing. 'It's going to be all right,' her partner said. Lorna could see her panic, the whites of her eyes.

'Move back please!' The woman from the desk and a man

wearing an armband had arrived. The woman knelt, pulled the girl's skirt down over her knees, leaned over and spoke to her. Whatever she then relayed to the man, he straightened up and mounted the steps to the stage. The silence was such that they could all hear the tap of his steps. He approached the microphone, no showmanship in his suit or his gait, only urgency.

'I'm going to have to ask everyone to please collect their belongings and make their way out,' he said. When Lorna turned towards the door, there was unbrawny Paul, sombre and neat, in his epaulettes and his sunglasses.

They had a run on tea. On the other side of the counter was a pool of upturned faces, a few with heavy-lidded eyes, a few exhaling pipe or cigarette smoke. As each person peeled off, they found a lantern to stand under and blew into their cup. Seaside attractions, the food kiosk and the white criss-cross frame of the slide beside the jetty had sunk into darkness. Lorna still couldn't quite believe what she'd seen. Was it God's work? She couldn't believe the girl had asked for it. 'She was only dancing,' she said, but neither Paul nor Bill had offered any judgement.

'Have they got a first-aider?' Bill asked.

'I don't know.'

'I'll just check.' He stepped down out of the back of the van. Paul put a fresh teapot in front of Lorna.

'Who was that bloke you were dancing with?' he asked quietly. A bus of dance-goers roared past. When it had gone her head felt clearer.

'He works at the mill,' she said. A siren wailed and lights flickered through the gnarled pohutukawa branches.

'Well.' Paul turned away from the subdued queue. 'You've

been a great help tonight,' he said. 'Getting stuck in, that's what it's all about.' Lorna poured tea into the remaining cups. You either helped, she realised, or you needed help. They hadn't had any smart alecks at the counter since the accident. Never mind the gospel and the preaching; someone had to keep their wits about them in the midst of all the excitement.

Paul got up to give testimony at their service in Birkenhead the following morning. Isaac was still too young to sit with the children for Bible study, so he was sitting on Lorna's lap, shuffling her dad's keys around on their ring. Every so often Isaac would jerk his head around to see if she could offer any entertainment, and when he did there was a kind of reverberation in his body afterwards. She wasn't supposed to encourage him so she kept her eyes in front. Her timbrel was lying flat on the floor under her seat; she'd learned her lesson one Sunday when she'd kicked it out from where it was leaning on the leg of the pew during an especially weighty silence.

At the lectern, Paul was flanked on either side by the corps and territorial flags. As usual he had his glasses on. 'My mother died when I was thirteen,' he said. 'My father, who is a greengrocer, used his savings to send me to boarding school.' The listeners took on an extra stillness. He was reading off a piece of paper. Lorna wondered if he ever got nervous. At boarding school he had been picked on, he said, and had spent more and more time in the workshop building a model motorboat. He had aimed to run it on the school lake and earn the respect of the other boys.

'Poor thing,' Lorna's mum whispered. Isaac squirmed when he heard her voice, but Lorna was too focussed to pay much attention. Paul lifted his head from his notes.

She couldn't tell where he was looking.

'Our manual trades teacher taught me how to do the welding,' he said, 'but he only had one decent pair of goggles, and sometimes I couldn't find them. I began to get these pains in my eyes, worse and worse.'

He was lucky not to have lost his vision altogether, the doctor had told him. Not lucky, according to the school's chaplain, blessed—a blessing for which he should be grateful. Isaac gave the keys a shake, and when Lorna closed her hand around them he let out an experimental whine of protest.

'My father thinks he's lost me to the God Squad,' Paul said, 'but his idea of normal is drinking and avoiding people. I gained so much when I joined the Army that I wanted to acknowledge God's great generosity by serving Him in any way I could.'

Isaac was batting Lorna's hand, the one holding the keys. When her dad reclaimed them Isaac squawked loudly enough to puncture the respectful silence Paul had inspired. A knot of embarrassment formed in Lorna's stomach.

Paul looked up from the lectern again, this time straight at them, without a doubt. 'Hi Isaac,' he said. A murmur of laughter went up around them. The knot in Lorna's stomach loosened. She looked at her mum, who was smiling. Even her dad was smiling. Isaac had gone still.

'Isaac doesn't need to worry about any of this yet,' Paul said. 'All children are blessed.' Another, quieter wave of laughter.

Jim

He's out on the showroom floor in a suit, weaving his way through armchairs, couches, dressing tables and chests of drawers: a vast, nonsensical household. At least it's on dry land. He wouldn't go back down that shaft for double the wage, whole thing gave him the heebie-jeebies. He spots a lady crossing the floor in his direction, not stopping to browse but gunning for him. Something in the tilt of her chin and how tightly her elbow pins her handbag against her coat deters him from intersecting with her. He's seen her before. Correcting a balls-up is more than he wants to do before he nips across the road for his lunch; as it turns out, something urgently requires his attention in the back room.

He stops, measures a chintz armchair and sets off on a different trajectory. In the meantime, she's gained ground. In his haste he collides with the cabinet in their lounge-room exhibit.

The china inside jingles in protest. He presses on.

'Excuse me.' She is within earshot. The voice isn't familiar but he can't be expected to recall every bird's chirp. He can only credibly claim not to have heard her once. He reaches the aisle. Phil is frowning at a clipboard in front of the office.

'Excuse me.' She's no more than three feet behind him. She must have run to catch up. He prepares himself to be to be surprised to find her there.

It isn't the same woman at all. This one has had a cleft palate repaired. Their coats and shoes all look so similar. 'Hello Madam.'

'Has someone bought it?' she asked.

'Bought the—'

'The chair you were just measuring. That's what I'm here for.' Jim's never liked chintz before but for the moment he's ready to swear by it.

'As far as I know it's available,' he said. She looks happy. He's made her happy, that's a turn-up for the books. 'My colleague here will be able to help, if you follow me.'

He celebrates not having buggered up her order at the Criterion, his favoured method of decompression by far, and by the time five o'clock rolls around he's found something else to celebrate. A person could never say of Jim that he doesn't know how to count his blessings. One blessing per jug is the going rate. 'Here's to the Prime Minister,' he says.

To his left at the bar is a butcher, on his right an insurance salesman. Or it could be the other way around.

'They say you get what you deserve,' the butcher or salesman says. They both abandon their stations before Jim's second toast.

He has his own method for attracting the barman's

attention and hose. He jams a finger into each corner of his mouth and lets go a dog whistle. It irritates the rest of the jostling heads and shoulders, but they aren't unsympathetic to another man's plight.

His whistle also brings a shepherd over. By the looks of him he doesn't often get to dedicate himself completely to beer and he's taking full advantage. Jim hasn't known country folk to waste much. 'I'm taking a girl to the pictures after this,' the boy says. 'I'm taking her to *South Pacific*.' Jim bows, an attitude he thinks will evoke sage advice. Where the ball and heel of the boy's shoe are pressed into the carpet, pools of slops have formed.

'Have you bought tickets?' he says.

'Not yet.'

'You'd better buy some. They might sell out. What then?'

'I don't know.'

'To women,' Jim says. 'They say you get what you deserve.'

Usual scrum at the bar for last call. The dog whistle might antagonise them under these circumstances so he holds his jug out and hopes for the best. Forgets the toast in his relief. Instead gives his final nod to a raised flagon back in the empty showroom, on the most comfortable couch they've got, a deep three-seater in the dove-grey 'abstract' pattern. And it is just a nod, or a nod and an intention. He's beyond words.

★

Next thing he knows, he's cold, and exposed to too much space. There are too many passing cars and their whooshes are being dispersed over too large an area. Before he hauls his eyes open he has time to form a theory, and he isn't surprised, when he finally does, to see the back of a couch. He doesn't feel at all well. Owing to the later winter sunrise he might have as little as fifteen minutes before Mr Gill arrives. Judging by the wetness of his trousers, the cold patch under his hips and the pissy reek, it's time he got moving. He steadies himself against the onslaught of light and nausea, picks up his jacket, slides the flagon underneath the frill of an armchair no one has ever shown any interest in, and makes for the door. He meets Mr Gill beside the angle-poise lamps.

Katherine

The driver slowed, looking for somewhere to stop. Dawn lit the sky above them, but shadows still crouched at ground level. 'On second thoughts, drop me at pier three,' Katherine said. He pulled over, wrote her a docket and left her at the bottom of Queen Street with her carpet-bag. A sparking trolley bus delivered onto the footpath the workers who would fill the juice tank under the giant orange on the Custom Street corner and open the doors of Pies, Pasties and Savouries beside it. The early birds would be arriving at the *Herald*, further uphill: bustling in, yanking the lift door closed behind them, certain young men—from the sports desk especially—rumpled and smelling of alcohol, not paying the least bit of attention to the typists removing their gloves and preening for the walk from the lifts to their desks, not for the moment at any rate.

Katherine missed the office from which she had compiled the 'Girls and Boys' page. She missed the letters from readers, their spelling mistakes and dried flower arrangements and the oddments they sometimes sent her (once, famously, a baby tooth in a chocolate wrapper). Every now and then a young reader had even appeared in her doorway. He or she would be accompanied by a mother and would be rigid with best behaviour, their shoes clean and their shorts or dress pressed, and Katherine would have to decide how she might live up to their expectations in the few minutes she had available.

She had an impulse to buy cigarettes after she closed the car door, her first for some time. Editors had all advised her much the same when it came to the Rotoroa home. The men needed all the help they could get, along with the good faith of the tax-paying public. The best way she could help them was by applying her trademark energy and enthusiasm. It had always been thus and thus it would ever be.

She threw down her cigarette end and stepped forward to look for traffic, but her foot met air and she stumbled. Without the agility to catch herself, she pitched forward and landed awkwardly on her hands and knees. After the shock of the unyielding asphalt, her first thought was cars, but a young woman approaching on a bicycle had seen her and dismounted. She waved the traffic past and leaned her bicycle against the nearest power pole. Katherine ascertained that her knees were sore, probably bruised, and the heel of one hand in particular, her right hand, which had taken most of the weight. For a moment she couldn't think how to arrange her limbs to get up.

'Lean here.' The woman reached down and with one arm she half supported, half lifted Katherine to standing. 'Must've got a nasty fright.'

Once Katherine was righted, and at eye level with her, the strength returned to her legs and she let herself be guided to the footpath. 'What a stupid thing to do. I'm all right now,' she said. She checked her knees. The stockings were intact; her skirt had protected them.

'Let me look at that for you.'

A patch of skin on Katherine's hand was rucked up and blood was beading in a few spots, but none was flowing. 'I need to get to the wharf,' she said.

The young woman took each of Katherine's hands in turn and rotated the wrists. Feet planted, nose pointed down at her work, glossy hair clipped short around her ears, she was as efficient as a mechanic would have been, checking the spark plugs in an engine. A young man would notice her soon and that would be the end of it. 'Turn circles with each of your feet for me,' she said. Katherine took hold of the arm she offered and did as she was told.

'I chose a good time to take a spill,' she said, 'just as you were passing.'

'Now.' The woman looked Katherine square in the eyes—hers were a surprising, warm brown—and spoke with practised concern. 'How are you feeling in yourself? Where are you off to today?' It had been long time since Katherine had received such frank eye contact, and she was appalled to feel a shifting in her chest, as though something was dislodging.

'I'm annoyed to have caused such a fuss,' she said. 'Otherwise I'm fine. Thank you for your concern. I'm meeting the Salvation Army.'

'You'll be in safe hands then.' The woman took hold of the handlebars of her bicycle and wheeled it back onto the road. The city had become treacherous, everybody hurtling about.

———

The *Mahoe* tilted back and forth in the fresh morning chop at the wharf. She was perhaps sixty feet long and coated in smooth white paint that looked new, or new-ish, and trimmed in sky blue. Alongside was the sombre profile of a man in the distinctive black uniform, who must be Lieutenant Hendry. He greeted Katherine and took her bag from her left hand. She held the other hand at her hip, palm upwards. The sun had not long appeared but the lieutenant was wearing sunglasses already. 'What have you done?' he asked.

'It's nothing.' She lifted her hand and brushed away the few tiny stones lodged in her skin. 'If you've got a bit of Dettol or something.'

'My wife will put something on that. After you.'

Katherine stepped aboard amidships, placed her good hand on the rail and lowered herself onto the transom. The lieutenant followed. 'Are you comfortable there?'

'Good as gold,' Katherine said.

He made his way to the wheelhouse. The smell of saltwater was familiar, the perching gulls, and the view back at the city. This was only the latest sunrise of many, but far superior for the prospect of being out on the water.

A girl approached in one of the Army's antiquated bonnets. The dark-blond hair that peeked out at the edges was cut short. She had a look of bare-faced practicality, none of the sheen or shapeliness that would be called pretty. 'Hello, I'm Lieutenant Lorna Hendry.'

'Katherine Morton.' Katherine was getting worse at judging age, but in this girl's case the leap from playing house to keeping house must have been very short indeed.

'Have you hurt your hand?'

Katherine turned it over. 'Just a plaster over this bit will do.'

After Lorna had put the dressing on she crossed her legs and folded her arms. She wasn't prim exactly. Tense, yes. They both looked out across the piers, towards the darker skies of the western harbour. 'I'm told the wind might pick up this afternoon,' Katherine said. The blood pulsed through her stinging hand.

'Do you get seasick?' Lorna asked. She turned her lips under. It was nerves, Katherine realised. She was nervous.

'Never have yet.' Katherine had spent a good deal more time on board than this sprite had, no question.

'I read some of your articles about the island when I was training,' Lorna said.

Katherine was touched. 'There's always a need,' she said. 'That's why I keep coming.' She rather coveted the chinstrap on the girl's bonnet. She herself had resorted to tying a scarf under her chin.

The wharf and Quay Street gradually drew away and the passengers lined up port-side to see the bridge in progress: great girders growing out from the north and south shores and men crowding over them, overseen by floating cranes, made tiny in the blue expanse. A fresh breeze skimmed past, gentle yet hurrying along with sounds and smells from the city until they were defeated by distance. At the stern, water churned through the ship's propellers, turned inside out and rejoined itself. They motored past a fleet of optimists racing, sailors scrambling and ducking, sails flapping and snapping taut. They passed through the sights of the gun emplacements at North Head, and the Gulf opened out before them: a different territory, where barrel-bodied petrels coasted by at close range. For an hour Katherine took in the refreshing wind, together with two tradesmen who were smoking over a pegboard game, and a patient accompanied by a court officer. Then she joined the boat-master in the wheelhouse and, with the help of a handrail bolted to the cabin wall, enjoyed the motion of the boat under them, the green suede and shadows of the islands they approached and passed, sometimes a spit where lonely trees grew. She didn't find much of interest in her *Illustrated Weekly* amongst the Brides of the Week, Chocolate Drop Pancakes and an epidemic of neuroses in America.

Rotoroa started small in the scale of all they had seen that day. It was a short string of land that grew as they zeroed in until at last they were confronted by Home Bay at close quarters. Little ever changed in this view, not the two headlands that enclosed the bay, one covered in bush, one grassed; nor the impression created by the rolling paddocks, the animals' pens and outbuildings, that it might have been a farm on a lake. Only the accommodation block set back on its slope was imposing, and even that became a curiosity when one was close enough to make out its corrugated-iron cladding.

In the melee of disembarking, greetings, tying ropes on and the team of men, weathered but willing, waiting to help unload, the superintendent's wife introduced herself as Claire McCallum. She was a substantial sort of person with broad shoulders, a long face and neatly set hair, but she was suffering somehow, her eyes and nose red.

'I'm so sorry. Hay fever.' She stepped back, turned aside and sneezed into a handkerchief. 'There's a lot to do but I'm just not'—she turned away and sneezed again—'not managing very well.'

'God bless you.' Katherine tried not to let on as the motion of the boat worked itself out of her nerves.

'Does the Bible say something about best laid plans?' Claire McCallum asked, then sneezed again.

'That was Robbie Burns I think.' Katherine left her alone for a few moments and watched the chain of men unloading. The donkey on haulage duty stared at the ground.

'Miss Morton, I'm Bob McCallum.' The new superintendent would have been in his fifties, with a stocky build and a tan. He was an administrator with a history, quite unlike the more severe superintendents she had met in the past. 'How do you like the *Mahoe*?' he asked.

'She's marvellous isn't she?'

'What did they have the last time you were here?'

'I don't think they had anything. I came on the *Coromel*'s route.'

'Well, I'll speak to you soon. The ladies have got some afternoon tea ready.' He left them to greet the patient who was waiting with the court officer and his wife pointed to the cart.

'Let's follow your bags.' Claire McCallum was putting a brave face on, but the glory of the day—the sun, the proliferation, the drift of seeds and pollen—was offending her senses.

Claire McCallum presented her two children (clean knees, wide smiles) to Katherine and showed her to the guest room, a different one from last time. By way of settling in, Katherine put her bag down on the spare divan. Through the east-facing window was a striving, spindly primrose and hanging on the wall above the bed Psalm 30:5. *Weeping may endure for a night, but joy cometh in the morning.* In the wardrobe was a spare blanket, a hot water bottle and a shoe brush and in the corner of one of the desk drawers was what looked like a half-sucked lolly, stuck to a piece of ripped paper and forgotten.

Her hosts had the radio on when she joined them in the front room for dinner. (Selwyn Toogood, typically rousing: '*Speak up now, don't be shy.*') The children were hugging their knees on the carpet, presumably forced there by the irritating grown-up chatter. Once the radio wouldn't have been switched on in company in the first place; once there wouldn't have been a radio.

A familiar view of Home Bay was spread out before them. ('*Margaret.*' The voice was tremulous.) The vantage point afforded them only the backs of buildings—the back of the accommodation block, for example—but the entirety of the bay itself.

'Golly, look at that.' Katherine was struck by it all over again.

'One of the patients has the best view,' the captain said. 'He's built himself a seat on Pakatoa Point.' ('*Here it comes, for the Remington Electric Shaver. Your husband will thank you for it.*') 'The generator here wouldn't cope with these gadgets,' the captain said.

Claire McCallum put two steaming dishes down on the table and pointed to the copies of *The Crusoes* Katherine was holding. 'Miss Morton has brought books for the library.'

'We had a sparrow in there last week,' the captain said, taking the copy Katherine held out. 'Flew in when the window was on the latch and couldn't find its way back out. Messed everywhere.'

'On the books?' Katherine asked.

'The books, the walls, the floor. Gave Claire a fright when she opened up the next day. Almost flew into her face.'

'Their panic is contagious, isn't it?' Katherine said.

'Awful,' Claire McCallum said. 'We're ready to sit around. I'll be back in a moment.' The room went from sunshine to shadow and back again.

'Hard to imagine how they survived,' the captain said, flicking through the pages. Weeks and months of Katherine's life slipped out under his thumb. 'Bell was single-minded, wasn't he?'

'But what adventures they had,' Katherine said. 'The daughter Bessie is one of the most cheerful people I've ever met.' She didn't mention the final dairy entry by the son, *Sunday Island has treated us very badly and I am not sorry to be leaving*, which had no doubt been slanted by the storm that had destroyed their house.

'Well, we're honoured to have these copies donated by the author. And signed to boot,' he said.

Claire McCallum had returned, and stood behind the laid-out table with her hands resting on the backs of two chairs. 'Time to get these two up.' She nodded to the children.

Her husband raised his voice. 'That's enough now,' he said. 'Time for dinner.'

Most of the patients were on the lawn smoking in the sun when Katherine's group approached the main block for the screening. For all its length, the building was homely. Its corrugated-iron cladding called to mind the barns and sheds of the back country, and was painted the same white and red as Northland churches. They continued inside to the dining hall, where chair legs made a squealing racket on the wooden floor. A handful of older patients had taken the first seats available and watched the preparations absent-mindedly. They appeared to be in Katherine's age group, though some might be a good deal younger. And there were bound to be more insidious problems that went unseen, bless their souls: shellshock, or dreadful growths in their livers. Light leaked through the gaps between the curtains and window frames. On the western side they blazed, like tears in the dim fabric.

She chatted to Claire McCallum in the front row while the seats behind them filled up. They spoke under their breath at first, but got louder and louder until they were almost shouting, by which time they were calling each other by their first names. Katherine would have liked to ask Claire which of the men were furthest from home, but somebody was tapping her on the shoulder.

She wasn't accustomed to such casual touch. The girl from the *Mahoe*, Lorna, was leaning forward from the row behind, her husband sitting beside her. Katherine greeted them both. Was that all? No, that wasn't all. 'I wondered if you'd like to join us, or join me, for morning tea tomorrow,' Lorna said. Her husband didn't meet Katherine's eye. It seemed a rather loose arrangement.

'That's very kind,' Katherine said. 'I'm not sure if I'm supposed to be anywhere at that time. Excuse me, Claire?'

'Yes?' Claire gave no sign of having heard the girl's question.

'Mrs Hendry has asked me for morning tea tomorrow. Is there anything planned for me?'

'No, tea would be at our house otherwise.' She met Katherine's eye. Beneath them, the form seat shifted with her boy's swinging legs. 'Will you need to stop at the house between times?'

Morning tea needn't take long, and the girl had asked of her own volition. Katherine turned around to Lorna. 'That would be lovely, thank you.'

Able to settle back in her seat at last, she asked the boy, 'Are you excited about the film?' though it was evident that he was. He smiled and nodded automatically. A stripe of light painted the floor between them.

'Phileas Fogg rides an elephant and goes up in a balloon,' he said.

No more need for small talk when the projector whirred and the lively score struck up. The film was a spectacle, certainly, but very long and perhaps a little disjointed—they were in Paris, then a bullring, then the Wild West. It was true that she rested her eyes for a few moments once or twice, and that in those moments she saw the cone of Rangitoto from the taxi window, the wake widening behind the *Mahoe* and the island's tree-lined arm reaching out to gather them in, but she hadn't actually fallen asleep, she didn't think.

Jim

He put the shears down and rolled his shoulders, rolled his head. A ten-year-old could have done the same work, and he was willing to bet the ten-year-old wouldn't have had knees that cracked and a shoulder that played up. Behind him, the lawn sloped up mildly, putting him in a grassy dip. A lavender bush hummed with bees. He didn't bother them and they didn't bother him. Mrs Mac opened the kitchen window. 'Would you mind helping us for a moment, around on the front porch?'

'Rightio,' Jim said. She didn't waste any time closing the window again. Some dimwit had planted the lavender directly underneath.

The back door opened and their girl materialised on the step holding a piece of paper. She was all dark curls, big teeth and spindly legs, and half paralysed with reluctance. The door was left open. 'We have to do a school project,' she said.

'Hard old life, isn't it?'

'It's to learn about someone,' she said.

Jim laughed, but she only continued staring. 'Is that a fact? And you want to learn about me?'

'Mum said it couldn't be about her.' Barefaced honesty, kids were the maestros.

'I see. It's bloody proximity I've got going for me, is it?' He expected Mrs Mac to rescue her chick from his swearing, but the doorway remained empty.

'Are you unsaved?' the girl asked quietly.

'I might be unshaved.'

'No, *unsaved*.' Her teeth sat on her bottom lip when she wasn't talking, as though they were trying to sneak out of her mouth.

'Am I a Holy Willy, you mean?'

'What's that?'

'That's you. You're a Holy Willy.'

'No I'm not.' She bent down and put the piece of paper on the step with a pencil from the other hand. 'You may wish to fill in your information yourself.' Jim had a fleeting desire to grab hold of her arm, give her a fright, but an impulse or premonition had winged the girl's feet and she was off inside.

There were typed instructions at the top of the page. 'You will need the cooperation of your chosen person. They may wish to fill in their information themselves.'

The list began:

Full name and place of birth
Jim picked up the pencil and wrote underneath, 'Jesus of Nazareth, 25/12/0000, Bethlehem.'

Occupation

He wrote, 'Messiah (formerly carpenter).'

Write 15–20 lines about this person.

She had started, 'He does the garden.' That might very well be true, in the broadest sense. He left it as it was.

'Doing some paperwork?' It was Lieutenant Hendry with the journalist. Jim found himself being stared at by his second female in a row, this time wrinklier. She looked strong for an old woman. Taller than Hendry, quite a square jaw, creases running from between her eyes up her forehead.

'It's for the girl,' he said. 'A school project.'

'Hello again, Jim,' the journalist said. 'Could I possibly commandeer him for a few moments?' she asked Hendry. 'Jim, would you mind?'

'How are you getting on here?' Hendry asked.

'Almost done,' Jim said. He didn't much like the way the old lady was eyeing him, but it would get him out of the gardening for a bit.

Mrs Mac appeared in the doorway. Quite the parley, this was becoming.

'Miss Morton's going to have a chat to Jim,' Hendry said.

'That's good,' she said. 'How are you getting on with your questionnaire?' she asked Jim.

'Actually, I couldn't borrow a rubber could I?'

'Of course.'

Alone on the porch, he and Miss Morton looked at the water they could see between the fuchsias, where the steps led down. A patch of cloud above the bay was lit from behind, whiter than the rest. As if Jim's fate wasn't already sealed, a shaft of sunlight broke through. Even he remembered the pictures in the Bible.

'Look at that,' Miss Morton said. 'If that isn't a divine presence.'

He let it go. He was sitting on the Super's porch partaking of his wife's baking. Rich were the rewards of religious reflection.

'I understand you're married with children, Mr Brooks?'

'She probably wants to be shot of me.'

His wife would be worrying. If she stopped worrying she'd have a ball: the place to herself to keep tidy and a baby that could sleep as much as she liked. It was the boy needed an eye on him, or he might cling to her too much.

'A father and a mother should be together if they can, surely?' Miss Morton said. 'What does she do in her spare time? Is she involved with a church?' She had a way of holding her eyebrows up, like a primary-school teacher with a kid.

'She sews things. Used to sew things.' It was the first thing that popped into his head.

'Yes of course, for economy. Clothing for the children?'

If she knew it all already, what was the point asking him in the first place? As far as he knew, she did it because she liked it. 'Other things too, to put the onions in, pot stands. Couldn't get her away from it.'

'Why would you need to get her away from it?' Miss Morton asked. Jim got stuck into his second piece of ginger slice. He'd been sick and tired of talking to his wife's back. No, she didn't mind if he popped out. No, she didn't want him to bring anything home for their tea.

Neither of them said anything for a while. 'Well, one mustn't neglect one's obligations,' Miss Morton said. 'Why did you use the past tense?'

'Pardon?'
'You said she used to sew.'

Lorna

If Lorna hadn't been wearing her new uniform and bonnet, if her suitcase hadn't been waiting beside her, if she hadn't already been on her way, she would have broken down when Isaac wrapped his arms around her neck on the platform at the train station. She put a hand on his back to hold him in place while the blurs of strangers went past, each going their own way. A heavyset woman in a suit paced towards the end of the platform. A young man with a duffel bag stopped and looked around. In the main hall a newsboy cried 'pa-a-per'. She'd been so busy with the Youth Council, rehearsals and interviews over the past few months, she'd seen less and less of Isaac, but not to see him at all was another thing entirely. She wouldn't walk beside him from the bottom of the back steps to the chicken fence every morning, and watch him choose a gap in the wire to stick his wrist through, see him open his hand again and hold it open, a pudgy spread eagle, as though he were waiting for a gust of wind to blow the last few husks out of his palm. But she needed to live her own life. She needed a fresh start.

Isaac's grip loosened. He began to squirm. It was probably for the best. She passed him back to her dad and picked up her suitcase. They were siblings, she reminded herself. She'd watched siblings at school and church enough times to know that although they might ignore each other for long periods, they always found each other at the end, when it mattered. She began to pick out uniforms amongst the people on the platform, other cadets. They'd all had their names and photographs printed in the *War Cry*, this year's intake, the Faithful. Paul had sent Lorna a note of congratulations. He'd signed it, 'God's blessings'.

She could hardly see her mum and dad in her swimming vision when she hugged them. She didn't dare look at Isaac. He yelled as she set out walking. 'Lor!' A high crow. It was a call only the three of them could translate, and it was lost across the open span of the platforms. When she didn't turn around, he yelled again, more demanding. 'Lor!' He was behind her, but the tone was enough to show his posture, indignantly upright, and the beginning of a frown. It was only the presence of the other cadets that kept her moving in the right direction.

An officer met the cadets at Wellington Station and ushered them onto a trolley bus down Lambton Quay, with its steep walls of masonry and windows, and up again, towards hillsides where thin houses clung on, to a natural valley and Aro Street running into it. *I am the way, and the truth, and the life.* Lorna knew full well that they would go out amongst the needy in the bus shelters of Courtenay Place, hold open-air meetings on Cuba Street and sell the *War Cry* in hotels, but to go the other way, to climb the steps to the William Booth Memorial College entrance, what a prospect that was. The building commanded a position above them: three storeys of red brick and white plasterwork with classical trimmings and tall, segmented windows, all balanced and symmetrical. When she was a child, Lorna would have imagined that an English or Italian lord lived there. Rather than interfere with this impression, the officer started up the steps one by one. The cadets picked up their suitcases and followed. The slant was so steep, and the overall effect so dizzying, that she didn't miss Isaac for several hours.

She opened her first testimony with John 14:6, *I am the way, and the truth, and the life: no one cometh unto the Father, but by me.* 'My family always sought to live under God's protection' she told the faces of the Wellington South corps in Kilbirnie, 'but we hadn't found the right path, the right way, at first. We were Christian, but still shiftless.' Her fellow cadets nodded her on in the front rows. 'As a young person, like so many others, I was unarmed against evil and was swept up in daydreams until I learned, in the Army, that I had to become involved in my own salvation, and the salvation of others. God saved me, placed me on the path, pointed me in the right direction, and now I live to show others the way.' She had practised it over and over again until she was fluent.

'Tell me about your call to service,' the interviewer had said to her. The high-collared jacket gave him a choked look, but his eyes were bright. There were three on the panel, two men and one woman, all living evidence of self-sacrifice, all humble and proper, but this officer had asked all the questions so far. She'd always felt as though she was looking for something more in life, she'd told them, and listening to the Intercessors give their testimony in Birkenhead, she had realised how many other people need the same love and acceptance she had found when she was brought to Christ. 'Giving yourself over to service is a life of poverty,' the interviewer had said, 'of self-sacrifice for a greater cause. Is your faith strong enough to sustain you?'

Lorna had no idea what she was and wasn't capable of. She thought of what Paul had told them. 'God will repay me in spirit,' she said, and she added, 'My joy is in abandoning myself to Him.' She had noticed that the other female cadets talked like that.

Best of all were the littlies, huddled on the mat for Bible study. Their curiosity was like a charge of energy. It reminded Lorna of her mum's old trick of plonking Isaac down outside her bedroom door on the padded seat of his nappy. He'd yell out, but his cries were still unintelligible then. They couldn't tell who he was calling to. Lorna was never conscious of the effort it took to get to the door and open it, not like other mornings. By the time she got there he would be deep into a complicated, swaying movement designed to get himself to his feet. 'Why was Jesus important?' she'd ask the children. Waving hands.

'He died on the cross,' one might say. Hands stretching up, some holding themselves under the armpit.

'He walked on water.'

'He parted the sea.'

'Do you know about the two Testaments?'

'Oh. Oh. I know. The Old Testament and the Nude Testament.' Giggles.

Every week the cadets straightened their hats, fastened their bonnets and zigzagged the blocks to the beginning of Cuba Street, through music from milkbar jukeboxes and past shopkeepers pulling their blinds down while a hubbub built up behind the doors of the hotels. A man ahead of them would hold the door open for Lorna and her comrade, and they would enter a very different church, packed with worshippers in variations of grey. With the noise and the number of men crammed in, the soldiers had to take a deep breath to fortify them for the charge. They were there to collect money, but they'd collect souls if they could. One would fire the shot and the other would shake the box for coins. 'Buy a *War Cry* and support God's work.' They'd told them at college not to be shy with the box, to give it an extra shake and wake them up.

Lorna held the box and her comrade Robert had the bag of magazines. The bag would get lighter and the box would get heavier, that was the idea. 'How's your training going?' one of the drinkers asked. 'My cousin's boy from Tauranga did it. Hell of a sacrifice.' His voice was more confident than your average man-on-the-street, less obviously local, and he used more emphasis—a lawyer or accountant probably, down from Lambton Quay.

'Going well, thanks,' Robert said.

The man pushed coins around on his palm, picked up two shillings, far more than the usual amount, and slotted them into the box Lorna was holding. He looked directly into her eyes. 'Indispensable, the work you do,' and that was when it happened: a brief squeeze on her bottom. It came as such a surprise, so utterly unrelated to anything else that was happening, and unremarked by anyone, that she didn't register a response at first. She was far too embarrassed to mention it to Robert, so all she could do was mumble a thank you and shuffle away.

It wasn't until a few minutes later, in front of a different group, that her cheeks began to burn. When she glanced back towards the man's leaner on the way out he was holding forth to the other men at the leaner, gesturing, his copy of the *War Cry* soaking up slops. Derelict dance halls and skating rinks in the East End of London had been Booth's first citadels, where he had convinced drunkards, fallen women and criminals to kneel at the mercy seat. 'Go for souls,' he'd said, 'and go for the worst.' These weren't exactly Booth's worst souls, the people they encountered on their rounds: they didn't seem to be criminals (whatever criminals looked like); women weren't allowed in the sports bars, fallen or otherwise; and you'd be hard pressed to pick the chronic drunkards out of the crowd that spilled onto the streets at six.

In her spare moments, and there weren't many, Lorna wondered whether she'd done the right thing by leaving. She read her mum's letters for news, to reassure herself that everything was all right at home. She worried about her dad occasionally. She read Paul's first proper letter in February, in her boxy chamber off one of the dormitory hallways that reached back towards the hillside. He had been posted on Rotoroa Island. Fancy the letter reaching her from there. She had no idea yet where her first posting would be, and no energy left to speculate about it, but to see his handwriting and hold the paper he'd pressed onto was enough to lift the weary drag off the evening. The North Shore's regional band had been asked to take part in the ANZAC Day commemorations in April, he said, so he would be visiting Wellington. He signed the letter 'Your friend in Christ'.

On her next afternoon off, she took work to the library. The rooms that faced the street, such as this one, were the more formal, with brass and wood panelling. For a while she tried to concentrate on her project, as befit the setting. She used her ruler to draw a border in blue ink around her table of contents, decided she liked the way it looked and set about drawing borders around the rest of her pages. Despite having the place to herself, she only stopped occasionally to stare blindly at the spines that lined the wall opposite. Rain had been falling, and she was far better off inside with the radiators. After she'd finished her borders, she opened the squeaking file drawer of press cuttings labelled M–S, and found a scrapbook under 'Rotoroa and Pakatoa—Homes for Alcoholics'. The Pakatoa Island home for women had closed in the forties. The first article she scanned was by Elsie K. Morton.

> When a woman falls victim to bad habits, she seems to fall deeper, to be more acutely conscious of her failing, than a man. And when she is so unfortunate as to lose her self-respect, she loses it more completely, and falls to even greater depths of despondency or recklessness than a man.

Even in the Old Testament, God told Isaiah, *Remember ye not the former things, neither consider the things of old.* John wrote in the New Testament that if you confessed your sins and left them behind, God would cleanse you of them. But Lorna couldn't take the credit for rejecting her sins; it had been Neil who had left her behind. Besides, she couldn't regret having Isaac.

Clouds were blowing past outside the window at the end of the table; they always were in Wellington, the wind had personality, could ambush you at will; but every now and then she saw something else, a flash of movement, small and dark. Birds, that was all. Birds were going about their days. She could only observe a blip in their journey. They seemed to have been propelled or thrown.

She found a clean sheet of paper. 'Dear Paul,' she wrote. She took a breath in and let it go. Her heartbeat sped up just forming the words on the page. 'Isaac is my son.' She put the tip of the pen back down on the paper and drew one of her borders around the words. She drew another around that one, then another, then had a surge of fright when she sensed a figure at the door. She turned the page over. It was her dorm neighbour, Faye, tapping her diary against the door jamb. 'Have you got a minute?' They had been paired together to organise a rest home visit later in the year. She was always energetic, Faye. She had better things to worry about than what Lorna did with her pieces of paper.

Back in her room afterwards, in a cave of white—white walls, white furniture, to help them see the dirt—she scribbled over the sentence she'd written, tore the paper in two, screwed up the pieces and threw them in the bin.

She couldn't tell if Paul noticed her in the dark before dawn on ANZAC Day, when they fell into formation below the lawns of Parliament House, everybody sombre and inward from respect, cold and lack of sleep. She could only make out clearly the faces of the men in the first row opposite at first, ignoring the southerly in their uniforms and medals, then, as light began to eke in, the second row, then the third.

She finally got to speak to him at a breakfast put on for visitors at the college. There was a mood of reunion in the dining area that day, with its alcoves and the view of steps outside the windows leading here and there at odd angles, the occasional burst of laughter and double-clasp handshake, and thank goodness, because otherwise she would have been too self-conscious to take Faye over to the table where he was sitting.

When he stood to greet them he was shorter than she remembered. Then he smiled, and the dimples appeared, and it began to feel as though they were having a reunion of their own. 'Haven't seen you in uniform before,' he said. 'You remember Bill.'

Lorna introduced them to Faye, and Bill reminisced about the brass fittings in the main chapel, which they all, as cadets, took turns to polish. Lorna and Paul weren't listening to him, particularly, but Faye tried to hold up her end. 'I counted them once,' Lorna heard her say. 'There were twenty-four.' Someone's leg, probably his, or it could have been Faye's, was jiggling the table.

Paul asked after her training and her parents while she searched the lenses of his sunglasses in their thick black rims and saw the ghosts of his eyes in shadow. She still couldn't read much expression in them, but she didn't need to, especially. In that public setting, he spoke to her intently. He'd been put in charge of the vegetable gardens on the island, he told her, the same piles of potatoes, carrots and silver beet he'd grown up handling in the shop. He had a work gang to manage, which was by far the most difficult aspect. 'It's hard to get them to respect me,' he said. During the pause afterwards he pursed his lips and twisted them to one side then the other.

123

This was a gesture of his he didn't seem to be aware of. 'Do you have dates for your campaign?' he asked, keeping his voice low, under the din.

'Yes, in late September.'

'I thought I might take my week's leave in October and come back for another visit,' he said. He gazed down at this plate, but there was nothing left on it to eat, nothing there to distract or delay. 'We could ask for permission to court,' he said. 'If you wanted to.'

'Nuggeting the steps was another one,' Bill was telling Faye. 'That took a while.' He stopped, not wanting to grumble. Nothing was onerous in the Lord's service; or almost everything was, to the extent that it wasn't worth remarking on. Lorna remembered him and Paul sitting in their lounge in Albany with Isaac yelling in the background. 'You're off to Dargaville on your campaign?' Bill asked Faye.

'Yes, in September.' Faye picked up and held the pouch she kept her glasses in, which was embroidered with the Red Shield. She also embroidered psalms for cushion covers. She'd promised the Faithful lassies one each at the end of the year. 'Then we're off to see the folk at Morningside in October, me and Lorna.'

'Will you have a band?' Paul asked.

At the mid-morning service, the North Shore regional band stood and raised their instruments. The onlookers were amassed in full daylight now, if not sunshine. Rain threatened, but didn't fall. The parliament buildings reared up above the cenotaph. A few streets behind them were the hulks of ships pulled in at the waterfront. Lorna was embarrassed at first by the sound the cornets made, a kind of comic parp it seemed to her, and by the tight grapes that formed in Paul's cheeks. The way he held the cornet in one hand when he wasn't playing, though, so loosely and unthinkingly; the way the other hand came up to meet it, all with so little fuss; none of that was funny. The piece they played was 'Light of the World'. The composer, who was a local officer, was famous, but Lorna was thinking about the words that accompanied the music. Paul had explained them in one of his letters. Christ was standing at the door to the heart knocking, he'd written, asking to come in. Lorna felt something in her chest, listening to the band play, while suit jackets flapped in the rows before the cenotaph, wreath bearers on one side, dignitaries on the other, but she wasn't sure that it was Jesus, despite having told everybody it was.

As the service reached its end, the wind picked up notes from the Last Post and words from the Ode of Remembrance and carried them off. The bugle player looked too young to have served in any conflict, whereas Lorna's dad had served in Italy and she had never known him to attend any commemorations, ever.

★

After the campaign, she spent a night with her parents. They picked her up from the bus in their good clothes. Her mum's hair was set in a kind of ball around her face and her dad stood with his hands on his hips. They looked like what they were: people who lived outside town and came in only sometimes. Isaac had turned two while she was away and had become a little boy, or the button-up shirt might have made him look older. His skin may as well have been translucent it was so smooth, and glowing faintly. Lorna crouched down to greet him, and he launched himself at her. In that moment he soaked up all the available colour and light. Everything that mattered in the world had been compressed into his two feet of flesh, and she held it in her arms.

The car ride home was all it took for her to be absorbed back in. By the time they arrived at the house, where the lavender and pansies were out and where brown, spent camellias lay on the grass, he was casual with her again.

Her mum fussed over *Hutu and Kawa Meet Tuatara*, which Lorna had bought him for his birthday. She promised to read it to him often, but he seemed to have a little motor running inside him that Lorna didn't think would let him sit with a book. He was far more interested in twisting the knobs on the radio when her dad wasn't watching, opening and closing the flue on the stove, and playing the game of running away if any of them approached him. Her mum had collected new creases between her eyebrows, strain lines. After fifteen minutes of being interrupted every few moments, telling Isaac, 'That's not for you,' and 'put that down', and 'listen to me, please', she finally took Lorna's old radio down from the bookshelf and placed it on the floor in front of him. 'I hope you don't mind. He's not doing it any harm.'

'How's your back been?' Lorna asked.

'Comes and goes,' her mum said. 'I've got some pills. The doctor says they might be able to operate on it.'

Isaac was singing—so far as Lorna could tell, that was what he was doing—filling in for the unplugged radio. When he noticed her watching he stopped and played silently.

'They're opening the Hamilton temple for public viewing in a few months,' her mum said. Lorna had seen an illustration of the design for the LDS building, which looked like a giant factory with a spire.

Her dad came in holding a bunch of carrots by their stems. 'One of these days we'll plug that radio in and split our eardrums.' He took the carrots out, ran water in the kitchen next door, and came back running his fingers through his hair. 'Did you tell her about the American?'

'No I didn't,' her mum said.

'Who?' Lorna asked.

'Barbara sent us a copy of *Te Karere*,' her mum said. 'I'm sure she meant well. Remember Barbara?'

'She had the husband with the goitre,' Lorna said. It had been Barbara's job to sweep the cigarette butts out of the Labour Hall on Sundays before their meetings. Bringing her to mind was like recalling something that had happened to someone else.

'Give that back now, that's enough.' Her dad lifted the radio away from Isaac's reaching hands. 'He only just got back to Utah. Someone told Barbara he was in trouble before he came.'

'The husband with the goitre?'

Lorna's mum eased herself forward. 'No darling, Elder Cowley. Come on now, let's all have a look at the garden.' She eased herself up. 'Here we go.' They both stood waiting for Lorna. She ignored the hollowness in her stomach.

'Come on, then.' Lorna spoke to Isaac, who had inserted two fingers into his mouth. 'How many different kinds of vegetables are in the garden?'

He forced his fingers into a complex gnarl and lifted them up. 'Four.'

'Do you know how many names we registered at our children's rally on Tuesday?' she asked.

'Four.' Everything was four at the moment, as far as he was concerned.

'Thirty-five,' she said, 'and one adult for reconsecration.'
He just looked at her.

After she'd admired the carrots and broad beans Lorna
spent half an hour rifling through boxes in her old bedroom,
uncovering chart booklets, the single 'Maybellene' in its
sleeve and a well-worn doll called Amber, stripped down
to her petticoat, before she found the sewing kit she'd been
looking for. Alan had given her the record on her last day at
the mill. She'd only listened to it once. Something about the
guitar, something raw, had picked her up and plonked her
somewhere else, plonked her on a chair in what sounded like
someone's garage, in a livelier neighbourhood than any she'd
ever been to.

★

The Morningside Rest Home, with its grand staircase in the
foyer, had been someone's mansion once upon a time, but the
pink workaday carpet looked as though it had been laid more
recently. Double doors led into what had been the ballroom,
and the other side of that opened onto a veranda, where two
residents read, lowering their books sometimes to watch as
Lorna and Faye helped the staff to set out chairs and arrange
the scones from the Home Leaguers on trestles. They greeted
the people who began to arrive: the men whose wives had
died who'd had no one to look after them; the women whose
husbands had died who'd had no one to look after them; folk
who were stooping and stiff; others who were sparkier and
more agile. Some patted Lorna and Faye's hands as though
they were standing in for their grandchildren for the day.

The residents liked the songsters well enough, but Lorna
could sense the anticipation build between 'The Light of

the World' and 'In the Army of Jesus', when the corps band filed in and sat down, with Paul and his cornet as guests. The players eased into the first world-weary notes of 'Abide With Me', and Lorna could see how the listeners were lost to reflection, no longer concerned about things such as where the belt of their trousers sat or how much rouge they'd applied. They had seen the beginnings of streets lights and electricity, gramophones and radio broadcasts. Six monarchs. Two world wars. They were time travellers.

She noticed one woman in particular wearing a satiny turban. The woman was in motion in her seat, letting herself be carried on the tune; her gaze wasn't focussed on the songsters or the band, or anything in the room at all, Lorna didn't think, but on something or someone in another place and time. Then she rose (it was a rising, not an awkward step-by-step exercise in getting to her feet; she found the grace somehow) and took up her swaying again, one standing out amongst many, and finally raised her voice in earnest. *'When other helpers fail and comforts flee.'*

The woman's brick-red twinset of cardigan and skirt didn't fulfil the grand promise of the turban, but she didn't seem the slightest bit worried, still seemed to be in her elsewhere, and the band played on, but Lorna sensed now that she couldn't remain there, singing alone. Her voice was thin and straining, and causing people to shift uncomfortably. *'Earth's joys grow dim, its glories pass away.'* A staff member started towards her row. All eyes followed. A few others in the audience began to sing, their voices as unobtrusive as the first notes on the instruments had been. The songsters joined in. *'Shine through the gloom and point me to the skies.'*

Never mind that the band members were playing their

instruments as softly as they could, the room was filled with sound now. Lorna could hardly hear her own voice. The staff member paused where she was. Paul looked up from his music at Lorna but continued playing.

The woman in the turban didn't seem to notice anyone else, not even when a handful of the younger or more able residents rose to their feet also. She might have expressed gratitude somehow for the show of solidarity, but she didn't do anything, not until, while the final line was being sung, she put herself in motion: without warning she wandered down her row, opened the side door and crossed the veranda, heading for the steps. '*In life, in death, o Lord, abide with me.*' The staff member, who was singing herself by that time, had to follow her.

Afterwards, Lorna watched Faye collecting the psalm cards people had sat on and left behind. She should start in the kitchen or stacking chairs. 'That went well, don't you think?' Paul was beside her. She couldn't read any sarcasm in his voice.

'They seemed to like it,' she said. She nodded towards the veranda. 'Especially her.'

He stepped in closer and lowered his voice. 'If we won her soul, I don't think she'd remember. Pack-up now, is it?' He stacked one chair on another, and those two on a third. 'I thought we could walk down the hill together.'

His cheerful dismissal of the woman irritated Lorna. 'Faye won't be long either,' she said. She regretted it immediately. His uncertainty was obvious in the way he stopped midway to the next chair and lingered, neither standing with her nor getting on with his task. Far from sensing any swings in Paul's affections, she got the impression that it wouldn't make any difference to him whether she said the right or wrong thing, or how she looked on any given day. It was a relief, but also made her feel oddly redundant, as though she could be anyone, as though a stand-in would do.

'I asked the captain if we could go just the two of us,' he said. He had waited with her for a bus back to college the day before. They'd sat there amongst the usual coming and going of passengers who studied the timetable, stood aside while the others alighted then embarked themselves. Somewhere in all that, he'd picked up and squeezed her hand. She'd looked down at his fingers covering hers. Eventually he'd let go. The only way she could avoid saying anything wrong was to say nothing, but that meant going unrepresented.

She looked at his glasses now and his Adam's apple. 'Okay.' The plan enveloped them in a kind of lightness, which took in the chandeliers and a lawn that descended into wispy white clouds outside. He carried on with the chairs.

They cut across Central Park near the bottom of the hill, where they passed a bench with bird droppings on it, and one occupied by a woman with a yapping dog. They kept on until the path disappeared into the shade of trees, into the dampness of earth and leaves and blackbirds fluting. After a footbridge Paul slowed, and Lorna slowed with him, until he stopped altogether and looked up and around, at nothing Lorna could see. Finally, he lifted the glasses off his face. He was squinting a little but otherwise his eyes were normal, just eyes: green flecked with brown, the skin around them slightly paler. She couldn't look into them for long at first, at the hint of unease there, as though she was invading his privacy somehow, as though they'd only just met. Without warning, without being able to help it, she felt tears coming. They spilled over, down her face. 'Sorry.' She wiped her cheeks with the side of her hand, but they kept coming, she didn't know why, unless it was because she couldn't tell whether or not she knew him, or what his feelings meant, if he didn't know her properly.

'It's all right, don't worry.' Apart from that, he didn't know what to say. He held his arms open. After a moment she stepped into them and rested her cheek against the wool of his jacket. Her arms didn't feel quite right at her sides but she was too shy to snake them around his waist. She had to adjust her footing until she was properly balanced. 'Whatever it is, God will help you,' he said. She could feel the vibration of his voice through his chest. God would help. That was a good solution for everything. His hands stayed where they were, resting on her back. 'I'm going to have to put my glasses back on, sorry,' he said. 'That light's getting quite bright.'

'Paul, wait.' She leaned back from his embrace. His squint was more pronounced now. 'Paul, Isaac is my son.'

After she'd said it her lungs felt empty, as though every molecule of air in them had been used up. Paul focussed his gaze below her eyes, on her cheek. He was still squinting, but it looked now as though he was trying to make something out, an object in the distance. The blackbirds were still twittering away, the sky hadn't fallen in.

'Who was—'

'He was a Mormon missionary. He denied it. Mum and Dad decided to adopt the baby.'

His expression remained the same for a few more moments, then he put his hand behind her head and pulled it gently towards his chest again.

'Don't you realise that makes your calling to serve even more momentous?' he said. She couldn't help feeling as though he was holding her not to reassure her, but so he wouldn't have to meet her eye. 'The Lord knows what's in your heart.' If God was there, and He did know, she was in trouble. 'You must have been praying about this,' Paul said. 'I'll pray too.'

'You're not angry?' she asked.

He held her with one arm and put his glasses back on with the other. 'It's a surprise,' he said, 'but I'm not angry.'

She could tell by the way he dismissed it that he wasn't going to say any more on the subject. In fact, neither of them mentioned any more about it until almost a year after they were married.

Jim

The boys are all home from Europe, the ones who are coming home, they were all welcomed in yesterday's parade. The mothers and aunts will do only the chores that are strictly necessary and then they'll be off around the houses to debrief over tea: whether Best Float and Best Costume deserved it, who wasn't there or didn't do their bit, the contributions of the local notables and how they were dressed. The husbands will dig a couple of implements out of the shed, bother something on the section for an hour then fall asleep over the papers.

Jim and his friends were too young to be drafted. At their unofficial clubrooms in Bert's garage, Bert relives the hullabaloo along Dee Street, from the military band and the soldiers themselves to the marching girls in furry hats and natty boots. Bert's mother had made hundreds of crêpe-paper flowers (she'd watched Jim walk along the path from the street to the garage today, bypassing the house, but she didn't wave).

Jim tosses his bottle cap into a tin on the floor between them. A neighbour is clipping his hedge outside, but it sounds as though he's working above their heads. This was where they'd started the day before. It was where most of their capers kicked off. Eventually the group had got separated.

'So Deidre Murphy's in her best frock up on the float,' Bert says in his hoarse voice. Jim likes Deidre, gets a good feeling even hearing her name. 'She's waving, everyone's waving their flags, and then from the frilly curtains under her legs, you see this head poking out.'

Jim joins in with the laughter, beginning to relax. He'd woken up that morning feeling as though something went wrong.

'What did you see under there?' Bert asks. Buttons, collars, questioning eyes, trails of smoke, it's all easier to take after the first few swigs.

'Who was that?' Jim says. After a beat they laugh again, louder.

Katherine

She met Lieutenant Hendry at the start of Palm Walk. The phoenix palms were still squat, only her chest height, but they lent that particular spot an exotic mood, somewhat like a military base in the Caribbean. The fronds of the nearest palm sprayed out invitingly, and Katherine took one in her hand. 'These will tower over our heads one day,' she said, 'or over your head. I will have moved on to a better place by then.'

'The patients are more likely to see them fully grown than I am,' the lieutenant said.

In the short time Katherine had been acquainted with him, she wouldn't have said he'd ever looked at relaxed, but against this backdrop, in his uniform and dark glasses, he was especially incongruous. That bastion of flippancy the *Truth* liked to point to a hopeless cycle whereby the men drank, were sent to the island to dry out and then relapsed again upon release, but Katherine thought of it as a sanctuary from earthly troubles, a place where healing was possible. To document the men's failures would only confuse the public.

'How long have you been posted here?' she asked.

'Almost two years.'

She gained the impression that in asking him questions she was upsetting his plans, but she was not going to be put off so easily. 'And whereabouts are you from originally?'

'My connections are on the North Shore.'

'I spent my first years in Devonport,' she said.

'Lorna and I got married in Birkenhead,' he said. The lieutenant was obviously choosing his words. His hands remained against his legs, awkwardly still.

'My brother is in a retirement home there,' Katherine said.

'Not the Eventide home?'

'No, Rathbone House.' This seemed to drive a wedge between them. She tried again. 'Your wife must have been a young cadet?'

'She heard the call early on.' He held an arm out along the walk. 'We may as well start at the vegetable gardens.'

In the past, the superintendent would have shown Katherine around, pointed out any renovations or additions and given her statistics to use in her article, but Katherine had been advised that Captain McCallum was delegating some of his duties at present. She respected his making the men his highest priority—he was their counsellor as well as a kind of mayor—but she missed the broader overview he would have supplied. There was no question that the atmosphere was less formal than it had been. The superintendent used to be a kind of prison warden. In the 1920s she had visited Pakatoa Island, next door. In a wraithlike flock the women had watched

137

her arrive, but they had scattered when she set foot on land. Nobody had suggested she interview any inmates, not in those days.

Several rows of cabbages, then carrots, then silver beet. The events of the world at large didn't disturb vegetable plots greatly, and these were much as she remembered them. Three men were in the garden, raking the earth near the far end. They were making their way across as Katherine and the lieutenant approached. 'How many are assigned here?' she asked.

'We have ten gardeners overall, five on vegetables. We're putting down potatoes, parsnips and onions at the moment, and trying to use corn and leeks.' She could smell baked soil, so perhaps it did need to be turned over after all.

'Good for the soul, gardening,' she said. '"The glory of the garden glorifies everyone", that's Kipling.' This garden and these gardeners might not seem glorious—their clothing, and the corrugated-iron fences were faded, shabby even— but they were labouring for the noble cause of providing for their community. 'I'm keen myself, but more enthusiast than expert.' Her garden at home was a half-wild mess of blooms, of varying heights and colours. 'I always think men are better on vegetables and women on flowers. Men like a straight line.'

Lieutenant Hendry pointed to the far left. 'At Christmas that row came up pumpkin, cucumber, potato, pumpkin, cucumber, potato, all the way along.'

'I've done that kind of thing by accident,' she said.

'You can be sure it was an accident when I asked them.' His tone was irked rather than condemning, she thought. These patients would be back in control of their destinies if they stayed sober. The lieutenant would always be God's servant. Katherine would have been less likely to hear about pranks from the superintendent.

'We grow lilies to sell, up there.' He was indicating the slope behind the office and hospital.

Zantedeschia. 'White and still as carven ivory,' Katherine said. It was a line from one of her essays. 'What a good idea.'

'They can overrun good pasture if they go wild. Have to be kept back.'

They joined the track past the accommodation block and two staff houses and out onto the open pasture. The lieutenant led them across paddocks where the cows raised their heads to stare but eventually, as he and Katherine got nearer, lumbered away, their thudding weight felt through the soil and clay. The climb had barely begun when it was over, a matter of ten minutes from Home Bay. The island's elevation was marked by a water tank and a half-inflated wind sock. Chamberlain's Island lay to the south, Waiheke to the east, and Pakatoa, no longer occupied, to the north. 'How many head of cattle?' Katherine asked.

'Something like fifty at the moment.'

Every now and then the breeze smoothed out the creases in the nylon sock and picked up a feather of Katherine's hair.

'A cow per man,' she said. She smoothed her hair for the third or fourth time.

'I suppose it is,' the lieutenant said. Rotoroa itself, its rounded promontories reaching out before them, was both idyll and institution, from its clay-baked cliffs to the whitewashed stones that bordered the paths in Home Bay and led out to the flagpole.

'They could each adopt one,' Katherine said. 'Like the mahouts with their elephants. They each feed one and look after it.'

'The mahouts don't eat their elephants, do they?' the lieutenant said.

'No. Good point.' She followed him when he started back. 'They wouldn't eat them if they were cows, either.'

He led her past the main block and the chapel down to the workshops and barns, past a man in a bloodied butcher's apron and another bent over a makeshift bench between two sawhorses. There were new holding pens attached to the shearing shed, empty of all but dried pellets, drifting wisps of wool and the waft of manure. The lieutenant pointed out the poultry yard in its new location—most of the strutting hens seemed to be Red Shavers or Leghorns—and they stopped to visit a feeding sow flopped over on her side. Her dirt-encrusted bristles gave way to swollen pink skin where the piglets scrabbled in close, pushing and nudging.

'It must be quite something to raise children here,' Katherine said. 'So much for them to see and learn.'

The lieutenant didn't reply. They didn't have any themselves yet, of course. All he said was, 'Hello, Betty', and this to the sow.

'During the time you've been here, have you formed opinions about what helps the men most, what they need most?' she asked.

His fingers shifted on the side of his leg. 'Most of them are fairly far gone by the time they get to us,' he said. 'It's difficult to gauge. We junior officers are only posted here for few years at a time.' The smell where they were standing wasn't pleasant, but the lieutenant seemed less inhibited and Katherine didn't want to rush him.

'Do you know much about these meetings they hold now, Alcoholics Anonymous?'

'No, you'd have to ask the captain or one of the men.'

'Is it God they need?'

He rested a hand on the top rail. 'There are fewer who find God than give up the booze.'

'All the same, you must believe it's He who saves them.' One of the piglets had been squeezed out, and was trying to barge its way back in.

'My father died last year, still drinking,' the lieutenant said. 'You can't force people, that's all, on either front.'

'That's not long ago. I'm sorry,' Katherine said.

'I lost him a long time before that.'

'And yet here you are.'

'Here I am.' It hadn't occurred to Katherine until then that he might not want to be.

The staff laid out rugs on top of a tarpaulin for lunch. Katherine had been supplied with a very low folding chair she wasn't looking forward to getting out of. She leaned back against the canvas with her legs stretched out in front, veins covered by her slacks. Men's Bay was beautiful, a scoop of blue fringed by flax, with a pohutukawa pitched forward at just the right jaunty angle. A tight flock of yellowhammers took turns landing on the pingao grass beyond the lawn. The patients were on clean-up duty or were sprawled out on their tarpaulins, the odd one or two on the edges. The fresh, flaking fish they had eaten for lunch was a privilege, biblical even, but it was only fair that the residents should enjoy God's bounty in this, His open-air cathedral, Katherine thought, when homespun haircuts and brackish water were their daily lot.

Claire McCallum had a copy of the *Free Lance* bumper quiz open on her legs. 'Next category, entertainment,' she said.

On the beach, one of the dogs nosed into an empty mussel shell left for the gulls. To breathe in the smoke from driftwood, this was normally reserved for happier occasions, more familiar company.

'How are you on these, Miss Morton?' Bob McCallum asked. Between the two of them they had given most of the answers.

'It depends,' Katherine said.

'Here goes,' said Claire. 'Oh dear: Buddy Holly, Ritchie Valens and recording artist known as the Big Bopper were killed in an aeroplane accident earlier this month. What was the Big Bopper's real name?'

Katherine was only vaguely aware of this kind of music.

'What were his songs?' the boatmaster said.

'I've only heard of Buddy Holly,' said his wife.

'They're all called "rock" something or other, aren't they?' Bob McCallum said. "Rock Around the Clock", "Jailhouse Rock".'

'J.P. Richardson.' Lorna delivered this with some confidence.

'That's correct!' Claire sounded amused.

'You have to be young for these questions,' the captain said.

'Where was the singer Elvis Presley born?'

'Not another one.'

'Tupelo Mississippi,' Lorna said.

'Correct again.'

'A Tupelo is a tree, isn't it?' Katherine said. She had seen one, and far preferred that to Presley.

'For a bonus point,' the captain said. Lieutenant Hendry had his hands clasped around a bent knee to stay upright and was watching Lorna. He hadn't answered any questions correctly.

For the meantime they had only each other to worry about. Everything would change when a baby arrived.

'Next,' Claire said. 'Who starred opposite David Niven in the film *Around the World in Eighty Days*?'

They all started as a group. 'From last night!' the boatmaster's wife said, but Captain McCallum frowned and shook his head to indicate that he didn't know, and Lieutenant Hendry resettled his gaze on his knees.

'Oh, Marlene Dietrich,' Katherine said.

'She was the supporting actress,' Claire said. They had to pass. The answer to the next question was Anna Pavlova. Katherine left it to the captain.

When it came time to shake out the tarps, she let Lieutenant Hendry help her out of her seat and then from the grass verge down to the sand. She was keen to see what the children had been up to, but there was nothing she could make any sense of in their hieroglyphs or trails. Nearer the water the footprints were deeper and the sand's surface slumped beneath her loafers. Only the oystercatchers had trodden lightly, leaving their delicate half-asterisks. The breeze was hardly brisk but she folded her arms all the same. In general her health was good. Minor ailments and aches lingered longer, but tended to pass.

A movement caught her eye and she watched the McCallum boy run with a bucket to the water's edge, wade in a few steps and dip it under. When he had reached his limit, he started back towards the picnic site at a ginger run but soon slowed to a fast walk, his eyes fixed on the slopping bucket. Childhood pleasures didn't change, no matter what messes the adults got themselves into. All this fuss about uncontrollable forces lurking in the subconscious mind. There was no evidence at that age. He reached the fire pit and Katherine watched while, utterly focussed, he tipped the bucket. It sent up a long, no doubt gratifying hiss, and he was obscured by the steam. He emerged again with his bucket, going back for more: the same sprint to the water with his arm extended, bucket held away from his shins; the same hobbled haste on the way back. She remembered his kicking shins in the stripe of sunlight the night before at the screening. With the image came a doubt, like a flash of something lost.

A series of shorter hisses from the fire this time, followed by an exhalation. The last seemed to come from behind her in the bay. It must have been an acoustic quirk of the cliffs because there was nothing there when she checked, only the water's surface, pewter rippling with silver, the distant backdrop of the Coromandel Peninsula, disembodied voices, what was probably the rattle of the bucket's handle. Then, near the reef, hardly a hundred yards away, two slick, slow backs rolled out, and two dorsal fins. As though turning complete circles they went under again, and the yielding water closed over them. Katherine didn't move. She had become a pair of eyes, detached from any aches or slights. The orcas surfaced again, in no hurry whatsoever, and one let out the clearing breath she had heard. They remained on the surface for longer this time. These distinguished envoys, in their dark bulk, were so at home, so oblivious to Katherine, but so commanding in their own right, that she knew she had been blessed. She and one other: the boy with the bucket was standing at the shoreline, still for once, staring, with the water lapping at his feet.

★

She had everything she needed in her guest room: somewhere to put her belongings, a bedside table and lamp. In the past she had craved novelty over comfort. Whether her accommodation was basic or well appointed, she had banked it all as experience, the planes of terracotta rooftops, tiles underfoot, a fan's beat and the hubbub of human beings outside. What distinguished this island was the absence of such things, the silence and profound darkness. The glow from her candle cast shadows over the walls, bent and primal, similar to others seen by countless generations in all of Earth's dark corners, no doubt. Alfie probably saw them in his tent the night before he died. There, as here, austerity would have been characteristic, the kind of depersonalised order that was necessary when one's thoughts were given over to service.

Lately, though, she'd grown fonder of her home comforts. Atmospheric the candle may have been, but the light it gave off was too dim to read by. She was accustomed to her double bed, a cache of bedsocks, her books, chocolate puffs, a spare blanket at hand. Having everything in its right place allowed her to navigate without thinking. Here, she had to lean down to retrieve each item from beside the bed. At home, her gaze often landed on the vine leaves carved into her chest of drawers, the same vine leaves that had been there while her parents were alive and before her brothers had married and moved away. Here, now, the furniture was all but empty and seemed to have been kept for decades despite being undistinguished.

She put on the bedsocks knitted for her by a member of the Women's Institute, which she still thought was a presumption, though she wore them. She could never have imagined in her tramping days that her circulation would become so sluggish. She would have sought out cold as an exquisite contrast.

'What's better than lying in a hot bath when it's raining outside the window?' a friend once asked her. 'A cold drip from the tap, landing on your toe and travelling down your foot.'

In her bed jacket and hair net, she thumbed open the fresh pages of the Forest and Bird Society's magazine. There was an article about the bar-tailed godwit, accompanying watercolour by Miss L.A. Daff; Lily Daff, that was, whom Katherine had met. She had died since. There had been a connection through someone Katherine was at school with, or a brother. She couldn't remember exactly.

In her journal she marked the date and sketched out the events of the day. She had kept her journals for sheer enjoyment at first. In loftier moments she had imagined gifting them for posterity, but more and more these days she treated them as an aide-memoire. Of the men she had spoken to that day, Jim had left the strongest impression, beginning when the roller had rattled open in the tuck-shop that morning. The queue of men had slid forward, and he had spoken to her. He was unusual-looking, imposing, with very dark hair. His shirt was too small and pulled at the buttons.

'I heard you on the radio talking about your book,' he'd said. His voice was light and bantering, didn't suit his physique. Half of the other men had continued gazing out at the chapel next door and half had turned their heads to hear. 'Are you addicted to islands?' he'd asked.

In her notes she had written: 'Torpedoed, Atlantic, 3x!' She had been taken on a tour of the dormitories, or of a selection of rooms with their doors open.

'Is that yours?' she'd asked one patient, pointing at the bowl on the windowsill.

'Mine, but not made by me. We used them at the Yokohoma shipyards.'

'Do you speak any Japanese?'

'*Nama biiru kudasai.*'

'What does that mean?'

'Draft beer please.'

At the craft display installed in one of the meeting rooms, a stooped, older man with hair sprouting at his top shirt-button had stood before a radio covered in pipi shells. 'What gave you this idea?' she'd asked.

'I copied it from one I saw in a milk bar in Paihia,' the man had said.

'What's your station, Miss Morton?' the captain had asked.

'It would be the Morning Concert on 1YA.' The patient had tuned the sound in, the Swan Lake Waltz.

'Frank was a patient here, now he works for us,' Captain McCallum had said.

'How's your life here, Frank?' she'd asked.

Frank threw off his response. 'I start fresh every day,' he'd said, 'working the steps.' Katherine had found herself objecting to the third step, which called on members to turn themselves over to God *as they understood him.* She felt they were being encouraged to create God in their own image. It all tired and saddened her, was the truth of it, the compromises people were called on to make. There was always the strain of making do, and it would be foolish to think the patients didn't feel every shortcut as further evidence of their insignificance. They needed to be connected to the outside world. They ought to be able to receive visitors.

'That's enough.' She said it aloud, closed the cover of her journal and bowed her head. She prayed for the patients and their families, such as they were, the staff and theirs, her own family, her brothers and their children, the great nieces and nephews. 'Bless them Lord and keep them safe from harm.'

Katherine's mother had given her the eyes to see God's majesty, had taught her where to look for him. In Katherine's memory, He was in a sunrise, on a tiny island at the mouth of a far-flung foreign fjord. She had clambered down from the deck of their boat onto a rocky outcrop to spend the night on the island alone, while a storm died. From her sleeping bag she had watched the moonlit outlines of threshing tree limbs, the mast swinging back and forth and the rushing clouds giving way to stars. She had awoken to see the branches and mast still and the blush of sunrise on the water, all dense and drenched in calm. Exalted, she had leapt from the rocks into the water.

'That reminds me of a night my sister and I spent,' Bessie Bell had said, when Katherine told her the story. They were on the veranda of Bessie's son's farmhouse, during one of their interviews. Never had Katherine seen such intricate crazing of a person's skin, yet Bessie had as much life force as any of the beasts on that land. 'I was nine and she was eleven,' Bessie said. 'We were coming back from goat hunting with my father and stopped to rest at one of the camps we used, which looked down into the volcanic crater and Blue Lake. We pleaded with him to let us stay the night there. "Can we stay here, just us? Please can we, *please.*"'

Bell had agreed, and had set off back to home base carrying the day's prize on his back, a live nanny for milk. It was Bessie's older sister who had come up with the idea that they should sleep in the Oven, which was their name for a cave beside the lake. Down into the crater they had ventured, past eruption-scarred trees. (Katherine had pictured them as she listened, the two tiny grubs of humanity, uncowed by the river of liquid rock beneath them, the earth forming and reforming.) They had curled up on the volcanic grit and in the arms of this most violent of earth mothers had slept the night through. 'What reminded me from your story,' Bessie said, 'was that when we woke up, we both sprinted like a couple of loonies and jumped into the lovely warm water of the lake.'

'How wonderful, the same impulse,' Katherine had said. 'Nature's baptismal.'

Bessie had begun filling her pipe. She had the habit of one per afternoon. 'I can't say it's God I think about when I remember that. It's my sister. I miss her.' The turmoil of the elements hadn't worked itself out overnight on Raoul as Katherine's storm had. The fire beneath continued burning in the morning, competing with the sun; it continued in sleep and wakefulness, light and dark, danger and safety. The girls had swum, dried off and made their way back to meet their father at the camp.

Katherine was in the habit of defending Bell. She was in awe of his vision. But Bessie's story, his failure to protect them, had troubled her. She wondered how their mother had suffered that night. *That we henceforth be no more children, tossed to and fro, and carried about with every wind of doctrine, by the sleight of men . . .* Only God knew and loved Katherine in a way no one else could. He knew she was the sum of her experiences. But here on Earth she feared an untended grave. When she closed her eyes she saw the orcas and she remembered, approximately twelve hours too late, morning tea with Lorna Hendry.

———

When she joined the procession along the jetty road the next morning, into the shade of the island's only stand of natives, she felt as though the island had reclaimed her and she were a member of the greeting party, though she wasn't in uniform, of course, and Toby the donkey towed her bag on the cart up ahead. She checked behind her, caught sight of Lorna and stopped to wait. As they walked on together she kept an eye on the potholes where rainwater had collected from the night before. 'I'm so sorry I didn't come to morning tea yesterday,' she said. 'I had an opportunity to speak to a patient, and got held up.'

'Oh, that's fine,' Lorna said. She spoke quickly, at pains to show how little it had offended her. 'The baking will come in handy.'

'It's probably for the best,' Katherine said. 'I eat more of that kind of thing than I should.' They stepped together onto the gently steaming boards of the jetty. The birds wished Katherine farewell, or she fancied that they did, the falling notes of skylarks over the paddocks above and behind them. 'You're coming back on the boat too?'

'To collect my brother. He's only three and a half.'

'Three and a half! He'll keep you on your toes.' It was best not to enquire. 'And how do you find it living here?'

'I had quite romantic ideas about what it might be like, I think. It was different from what I expected,' Lorna said.

'That's life, isn't it,' Katherine said, 'different from what we expect?' Lorna surprised her by laughing, and heartily. It was still girlish enough to draw the attention of the men milling about. 'Romance prefers to take us by surprise,' she added, not that she would know anymore.

'There they are now,' Lorna said. The prow of the vessel

had come into view, the means by which Katherine would be conveyed from this bright panorama back to concrete and crowds and eventually her hearthrug. She found she was reluctant to leave. As the *Mahoe* approached, they were confronted by the passengers on deck, who were strangers to Katherine.

On the jetty, two men who must be the doctor and magistrate shook hands with the captain while Claire smiled and waited to explain the domestic arrangements. In their suits and hats of muted colours, the two men were incongruous on a landing being lapped by water and sunlight. 'We're lucky to have Katherine Morton here,' the captain said. 'One of New Zealand's best known lady writers.' He introduced them.

'You would probably know me as Elsie Morton,' Katherine said.

'My wife has bought your book,' the magistrate said. '*The Bells on Sunday Island*.' He swiped at his dishevelled hair with his fingers and put his hat back on.

'Has she? Well, I hope she enjoys it.'

'My father heard several of Thomas Bell's petitions in parliament,' he said.

'Goodness me, did he?' After he'd left Raoul, Bell had fought for his rights over the island, time and time again, for the rest of his life.

'He thought Bell was mad,' the magistrate said.

'He wasn't the only one,' Katherine said. Men and boys and boxes eddied around them. Katherine had better be boarding soon, but in the meantime no one seemed much inclined to move on. The expertise of these men and the files in their briefcases qualified them to assess the health and rehabilitation of men who weren't likely to be healthy and weren't likely to have been rehabilitated. Whatever else the group might have been, at that moment they were partial to standing out over the sparkling water of the bay.

Jim

At the sharp end of the reef he squatted and tried to tear in half one of the mussels he'd brought with him, but the rind came away in one piece, leaving him with a falling-apart half, flapping open to show its guts, which wouldn't thread onto the hook cleanly. He tore another, holding onto the rind this time and giving it an extra pull to break it. Water rinsed gently through the caverns and crenulations beneath his feet and leaked back out. Gulls began to take notice of him, make passes overhead.

When he'd baited the hooks he planted his sandshoes, held his rod back, paused, and whipped it forward. The line whirred out high and landed short. He'd let go too early. He wound it in and cast again: gave the handle the extra flick with his wrists at the end. This time the rig sailed out in front and plopped into the water thirty feet away. He waited for it to hit the bottom then took in the slack. Much of his line was invisible against the cloud. Twice he felt very gentle tugs. He studied the tip of the rod for movement, but didn't strike.

The cicadas were still singing. All was calmness. No drama in the weather or the water. Even in a storm the swell in the Gulf would never send waves out to snatch you. He was remembering the game they used to play at Oreti as kids—how they would sneak up on the receding water then sprint away from the returning waves—when a fish took his bait. He struck hard. In his surprise he tensed up and wound in against the bent rod. In an instant, the tension was gone; not only the fish, but the rig and all. 'Shit.' The end of his snapped line floated somewhere between the third and forth guides.

Hooks, chain links and sinkers rattled in his tackle box. The sequence of tying up the traces was familiar, but he couldn't have been much older than fifteen the last time he'd done it. On the beach, two oystercatchers stabbed their red beaks into the sand. In a rock pool beside his foot were anemones and, when he nudged a stone in with the toe of his shoe, piqued crabs. He was alone and not alone.

Jim's father, an accumulation of wiles when he got old, used to complain to the magpie that hopped and flapped around the shed where he worked. Jim's mother, when she brought tea out, would stamp at it to shoo it away. 'No cake today!' it would say. 'No cake today!' The likeness was uncanny. Could have been a recording.

He made a few false strikes on his next cast, only jigged the weight of the sinker, yanking at nothing and feeling foolish for doing it, before he finally hooked a fish for his trouble. When he did, the reel wouldn't let him feed more line out, so he could only hold the straining rod and wind in on the slack. Each time the weight came off he thought the fish had slipped the hook, but it travelled erratically towards him until he saw colour through the water.

What he cleared was a snapper at least a foot long, pink, flipping on the end of the line. He didn't have a net, and could only think of getting it well out of the water so it wouldn't unhook itself and slither away. He swivelled the rod around and lowered the fish into a rock pool. Far from calmed, it slapped the surface and tangled the line around the tip of the rod. He put the rod down, bent over and tried to clamp both hands around the fish, fingers splayed. It took him a few attempts, but eventually he got hold of it. He pressed firmly with his palms and fingers and although the pressure was constant, and shifting, there was nowhere for the fish to go. Jim lowered the snapper towards a rock and slipped a hand away, but it worked itself into a crevice so he jammed a foot in after it, and crouched slowly. He watched the pearly scales for movement, for shifts in reflection. If the fish had been in better fettle it might have shimmied back out from under his foot, but its fight was fading. Only the tail flicked. By shifting his feet and reaching an arm out he could get close enough to retrieve his knife.

He drove the blade in above the eye and wiggled it back and forth, not sure if he was meeting the right resistance. A slow puffing out of the gills. A trail of blood leaked into the crevice, and when the eye finally took on its film half a minute later he pulled the knife out. A viscous string of something came with it. He lifted the relaxed weight of the fish, finally, and felt the inevitable anti-climax. The pleasure of eating it would be tainted by the kill. At home, the silver dollar gum would still be growing under the side of the house, roots driving in amongst the pipes. He didn't have any decent tools, or a picnic table for the kids to sit around out the back.

By the time he'd pulled the hook out, cut the tangled line, and packed everything away into the tackle box, a great deal of time seemed to have passed. The light was going. He hardly bothered with his foot placement on the way back.

Lorna

At college it had been Lorna who followed orders. On the island it was the patients who were up sharp every morning for breakfast and work sections: cooking and cleaning indoors, farming and labouring outdoors. Taking into account their work, twice-weekly church services (if attended), once weekly AA meetings (if attended), Monday sausages, Tuesday fish, Wednesday mince and so on, they had more commitments than Lorna.

As a wife, her ministry was limited. She spent most of her time at the weatherboard cottage assigned to Paul and her, where she used an iron range, boiled their clothes in a copper and left her food scraps out to be collected for the pigs. Every Tuesday and Saturday the *Lady Roberts* brought people, food and general supplies, including the illustrated weeklies and the racing papers. She learned that Elvis had joined the army and become a showboat in uniform. A month later they published a photograph of the Mormon temple near Hamilton. The caption said the Latter-day Saints had brought in marble from Italy and a baptismal font made in Switzerland. Strange events had occurred while it was being built, wrote Lorna's mum, quoting Barbara, whose husband had the goitre: rain clouds that divided and travelled around the site on just the day the foundations were being poured.

Some weeks, Claire McCallum would give Lorna the men's letters to read. She was to strike out mention of anything illegal or sexual, and any abuse or threats, but the letters were usually polite attempts to reunite with relatives whose patience had been tested one too many times already. Complaints and gossip found their way in occasionally. 'I'm so sick of chopping firewood,' one letter had said. 'If I look like dying here I'll ask for a funeral pyre to use up my quota.'

After she'd finished her devotions, while the Correspondence School mothers were guiding their children through their lessons, three times twelve and p-e-r-p-l-e-x, in good weather she took the washing out to the lawn behind the house where she could watch the birds and listen to sounds carry across the natural amphitheatre of Home Bay. Theirs was the westernmost house, halfway up the slope. There were two ways out of the back lawn—one through a gap in the hedge, which joined the track to the shore, and the other uphill to the paddocks and windsock above. On Saturdays, music carried over from the accommodation block and rec room, Jerry Lee Lewis or the less wild Everly Brothers. She stopped on the track one Saturday to listen to Buddy Holly's 'Peggy Sue', the beat of approaching war drums, and one of the newer patients, Jim, shouted down to her from one of the windows above. 'Can you dance?' She held a hand up to shield her eyes. He had thick black hair and bushy eyebrows. She assumed someone with a more exotic name had married into the family somewhere along the line. All of the patients looked as though they'd been around the block a few times, but Jim looked healthier. It might have been the hair. She wondered how long he'd been leaning out, watching. 'Too worldly is it?' he asked. 'No one ever showed you?' None of the others would have yelled down at her like that.

'*Then you'd know why I feel blue.*'

'I don't, but that doesn't mean I can't.' She was shouting herself, now, to make herself heard.

'Big talker, eh?'

Plunge and scrub, plunge and scrub. Pockets of air would billow the wet shirts and blouses in the copper. The vegetable gardens, where Paul spent a good deal of his time, were only a couple of hundred yards below the house. Lorna could be thinking of any old nonsense and he would come in off the track and snap her out of it. That was what happened in September, during their first week of warm days, when he appeared beside her with his hat in his hands. Something was wrong.

'Dad's died,' he said.

'Oh no.' She moved the washboard out of the way, shook the water off her hands and lifted her chair back. With her arms around him, she could smell that he'd been standing out in the sun or gardening. 'He's with God now,' she said. Funny that, embracing him, she should notice the farm manager's cat slink into view from the corner of the house, low on his shoulders. She quite often found sparrows on the doorstep, stiff and straight as though they'd died of shock in a convenient position for the coffin. Animals were the closest she'd come to death, before that.

'They think it was his heart,' Paul said. 'The butcher's boy knocked for five minutes, then went in. He'd had to wake him up for money before.'

Lorna had never met Paul's father, Arthur. In photographs, he was an inflated version of Paul: what he might have looked like if he had eaten more or spent more time on a bar stool. The dimples were there, but drilled into fuller cheeks. There were no clues in his appearance as to why the drink had got hold of him. His was exactly the kind of soul the Army wanted to win. When Paul had complained about the snails getting to the cabbages in the veggie plots, she'd suggested he write to his father to ask for advice. Arthur had never written back. 'What was the point in that?' Paul had said at the time. 'Why couldn't I just use the *Yates Guide*?'

She drew the kitchen curtain and Paul took his glasses off and sat down. She pulled a chair out to sit in front of him. 'I thought he'd say something eventually,' he said. 'I don't know.' No tears.

'You wanted him to say sorry,' she said. The tablecloth was outside in a pile, being dried into creases. Bare, the table showed its scratches, even in the dim light. Paul rubbed his face with both hands.

'He probably thought he did his best. I got fed, went to school, survived.' He'd had it almost as bad at school as he had with his father. 'Uncle Reg has started getting the funeral organised. He's expecting us tomorrow. We worked out the announcement for the paper.' She reached out to hold his hand. 'No one will come,' he said. Eventually he relaxed a bit and put his hand on top of hers. There had been times, with their fingers entwined, when she'd lost her sense of which were hers and which were his. 'Can't see myself being much of a father,' he said.

'You'll be completely different,' she said. He'd talked about this before, how he would and wouldn't be with his own children. They couldn't afford to get into it now, on top of everything else.

'Bob told me to come home for the day,' he said. 'I'll go and sort things out and come back for lunch.'

'Do you have to?'

'I'll just make sure they're all right down there.'

She lingered in the sanctuary of the kitchen, stared down at the pocked table and thought about what they would need for the next few days. The meat in the safe would have to be given away. It wouldn't cook in time for lunch, she didn't think. At least their clothes would be dry in time to be packed, so long as she pegged them up for the afternoon. That thought spurred her back to her task, back to the room, back to herself, and she realised that what she could see in her peripheral vision—black, folded arms—was a side-on view of Paul's glasses. She was used to seeing them on tables and benches at night, in low light, but not during the day, and definitely not when Paul himself was somewhere else. She ran out the door and down the back steps with them, and there he was on the other side of the hedge, his face naked in the sun. He was squinting, but so was she after the twilight inside. He seemed annoyed rather than pained.

'Didn't you notice when you got to the door?'

He held his hand out for the glasses and put them on, ignoring the petals of a white butterfly dancing in front of him.

'I'm a bit numb I suppose. I'll get a headache later.' She didn't need to be able to see his eyes to know she should stop asking.

If he got a headache that afternoon or evening he never mentioned it. They buried Arthur not in Te Awamutu with his parents but in a plot that had been bought for him by his brother, Paul's Uncle Reg; they'd been brothers in childhood and would be again in death, after a gap that had turned out to be the rest of their lives. Arthur had ruled out a Salvation Army service in his will, so the funeral was held in a modest Baptist church, with only the steeple and arched windows to give it away. Inside was the usual sense of time having slowed down, the faint waft of candles burning and the creak of wooden benches in a space reserved for nothing but worship and contemplation. There might have been no weather at all, but the dullness at the windows told them clouds were passing.

Lorna's parents brought Isaac in and sat with him in the second pew, behind where Lorna was standing with Uncle Reg and Paul, conferring with the minister. She said hushed hellos to them. Isaac had grown taller again in the six months since she'd seen him. His hair was cropped, and could only kink, not curl. She could see Neil in him now, especially in his mouth, with its full lips. Those lips proved something that seemed implausible to her otherwise. When the minister left them to take up a position on the altar steps for the first hymn, Lorna noticed a boy of about twelve slip in through the doors and perch on the last pew at the back. The butcher's boy, Uncle Reg told her. Isaac must have noticed him too, and decided he was the most likely one to provide a distraction; when the first notes of the organ were played he shimmied out from his seat at the end of their pew and walked the boy's way, tapping the empty pews on his way. She watched him go and sat down herself. He was probably better off at the back than up near the coffin. She could sense that her dad, behind her, was not so resigned.

She held Paul's hand while Uncle Reg spoke of his sister-in-law, Paul's mother. 'What a devastating blow it was when she was taken,' Reg said. He was quite different in appearance to Arthur and Paul, narrow in the nose, the shoulders and the set of his eyes. 'We don't know that Arthur ever found faith to help him through the hard times,' he said. 'We don't know what his thoughts were in the days and moments before he died, but God does, and God forgives.' Reg didn't mention what it was Arthur had found instead to help him through the hard times: he had been well on his way to alcoholism already when his wife died, according to Paul, who had turned down the opportunity to speak himself.

Even with little experience of funerals, Lorna knew the scattering of onlookers was paltry. The mood wasn't helped when her dad, after the final hymn finished, slid out of his seat and towards the doors, collecting Isaac by the wrist from the last pew on his way. She wanted to rush after them, but all she could do was stay by Paul's side while he thanked the minister and they waited for the sexton to come and act as a pallbearer to bolster numbers. She hoped her dad would remember that he had one more duty to carry out.

Uncle Reg lived in a house with a handsome veranda overlooking a reserve. He had vacated the very same house so Lorna and Paul could spend their wedding night there. Despite having prior knowledge, Lorna spent a noisy few minutes in his bachelor's kitchen opening and closing cupboards and drawers to find what she needed to serve tea and sandwiches. The tea strainer was in with the plates and the sugar was in the refrigerator. A good thing, then, that the only people to have come back were Lorna's family and the Engs, who had helped Lorna's mum at the bus stop. Mrs Eng was as fair as ever, but she had changed shape and wore smocks that flared out below her bosom now, to play down her pregnancy.

Paul joined Lorna in the kitchen when she was getting ready to take things through. 'Isaac's done well, hasn't he?' He'd been too distracted to notice the incident at the church. Since they'd got to the house, all Isaac had done was go around tapping the backs of the chairs. Paul wasn't to know that this was penance.

In the next room, Isaac paused behind the dining chair nearest the kitchen door. Lorna met his eye and smiled. He looked tempted to give in, but he managed to keep up his solemnity. It was as though by being forced he'd finally caught on to what the day required of them all. She gave Paul the plate of sandwiches. 'Offer one to Isaac,' she said, and nodded him on.

To Isaac, Paul was a pair of legs, then a face that swooped in from above. His expression went blank. Lorna watched Paul crouch down, raise a hand to his glasses and lift them up and down off his nose a few times. Isaac broke into a grin. He might have had a rough morning, but he knew a game of peek-a-boo when he saw one. Although she'd been the one to encourage them, Lorna felt left out. Isaac hadn't shown much interest in her this time, nor had he given her any of the cuddles she'd been looking forward to.

When she followed Paul in with a tray, she found them in

a ring of improvised seating: her mum in a straight-backed chair and her dad on a stool staring at the fireplace, regretting his temper by now, she supposed. Poor Isaac had no choice but to soak up all the adults' anxieties despite being oblivious to them. She remembered, then, what it felt like to grow up alone.

When she took Reg a cup of tea, he patted the settee beside him. It was rare for him to make a point of speaking to her. 'Listen,' he said. 'You and Paul won't be forgotten. I'll be looking out for you.'

He and Paul had cleared out Arthur's house together the day before. The Sallies might not have won his soul, but they would inherit his furniture. Judging by his breath, Reg must have thought he owed Arthur a toast for this disloyalty. They had come across plenty of drink at the house, Paul told her, as well as photographs. He had shown her one of his mother being ambushed by a street photographer, clutching her handbag with a closed-mouth smile. It always surprised Lorna how ruddy his mother looked, not the delicate girl she'd imagined.

Reg gave her hand an insistent pat. 'Paul's always been a harder nut than he looks. You must have some mettle.' Lorna felt a feathery tap beside her collar and turned around to see Isaac peeking out at her from behind the settee. She stood up. 'I'll take him outside for a few minutes,' she told her mum, whose seat was nearest. She leaned towards Reg. 'Don't tell Paul you've had a drink.'

He didn't reply, but he gulped his tea and reached forward to take a sandwich.

Isaac hared off down the hallway ahead of her and down the steps at the back porch. He found a shed first, which might hold any number of thrills and prizes, but there was a padlock on the door. 'He won't like that.' Lorna's mum had followed them, and was standing on the step behind her. They watched Isaac rattle the door more and more violently. It was hard to imagine him being occupied by an unplugged radio these days. Lorna's mum gave her a ball she was holding, and Lorna aimed it at the concrete beside Isaac, but it bounced high with a series of silly boings beyond the shed, down a set of steps and into a pond. A pond! That was much better. 'Who can find a stick that will reach that ball?' her mum asked. Isaac ran for the miniature wilderness at the bottom of the section.

'He reminds me a bit of you when you were little,' her mum said. 'Always keen on new places, new people, new things.'

Isaac aimed a damp flax frond at the ball, which slapped the top of it, useless. This was an old neighbourhood, three generations at least, plenty of time to accumulate water features and mature trees. Under the clouds, it was almost dank. Lorna sat down on the step. Her mum sat beside her.

'People are asking us about a baby,' Lorna said.

'I wouldn't worry just yet. They say to leave it a year.' Her mum held out a stiff-bristled broom that had been propped against the back wall. 'Isaac, try this.' When he didn't respond, she yelled again and waggled it impatiently. 'Isaac!' He started back towards them up the steps. She didn't meet Lorna's eye when she sat back down, leaning on the wall for support. Her hair wasn't set that day. She'd pulled in back into a bun.

They watched Isaac drag the broom as far as the pond. Lorna saw hazards everywhere he went, in the concrete steps and the pond for starters. She supposed it got easier to relax, the longer you spent with them. While he was trying to gain a useful grip on the broom's handle, he batted the ball with its bristles. It drifted straight to the edge, within easy reach, but he didn't notice.

'What about Paul's eyes?' her mum asked. 'Has he seen a doctor about them recently?'

'Isaac, it's there!' Lorna yelled. 'I don't remember him ever going to a doctor,' she said in her normal voice. 'He went outside in the middle of the day without his glasses and it didn't seem to do him any harm.' They waited while Isaac bent over the edge of the water, picked the ball up, steadied himself on his feet, then threw it back in.

'People get used to things,' her mum said. 'Speaking of doctors, they've given us a date in February for the operation.' She shifted position on the step. 'They're going to cut away a bulging disc.'

The thought of her in hospital was wrong, far too impersonal. 'Will that fix it for good?'

'They can't give me a new back. But it should be better.' Isaac picked up one end of the broom handle again. 'We could send him over to stay with you in February.'

The thought of being responsible for Isaac scared Lorna a little, but he'd adore the island. The skyline of Auckland, the cars, the built-up streets, the people: she'd felt removed from it all, being back, as though the island were another secret to keep. She wondered what Paul would think. He wouldn't be there during the day.

'You might be carrying your own baby by then,' her mum said. She didn't pick up on her mistake. 'Do you think Paul would mind?'

'I don't know. He might enjoy it.'

Her mum looked up at her. Lorna had been taller since around the time she got pregnant. 'I fell out with my parents when your father and I became serious,' she said. It came out of nowhere.

'Why?' The air had thickened with moisture. They saw Isaac, the pond and the trees through this grainy filter.

'Your gran said I'd grabbed on to the first thing that came along.'

Lorna's haunted, harried dad. 'But they liked him in the end,' she said.

'Their objections seem less important after a while,' her mum said. 'But in the meantime you say things to each other than are harder to forgive. Your gran said some awful things to me.'

It was a dreary day for thanksgiving, but Lorna realised she was lucky. Her family were all, together and individually, making continual adjustments to stay bound together.

Gales picked up that night. Lorna and Paul were restless, with so much working against them: Arthur's death, the wind shaking the loose window catches, the prospect of an early start and a choppy crossing on the *Lady Roberts*. Instead of sleepily half-waking if Paul turned over, and being soothed back under by the looming mound of his back, Lorna woke to full alertness, to the room and their place in it, the ticking of the clock. This was the room where they had spent their wedding night. For the ceremony she had worn a sash and corsage over her uniform, and clutched a bunch of dahlias. Faye was her bridesmaid (she'd finished stitching all of her cushions as promised—Lorna's said *Rejoice always*, the shortest verse after *Jesus wept*). Bill was in charge of the rings, and Isaac had worn his first tie. Lorna's father had walked her down to stand under the arbour. Only a few days earlier, Lorna had been commissioned as an officer in a crowded

Wellington citadel and urged 'onward to conquer the world with Fire and Blood'. In the months since then, she and Paul had established their habitual nightclothes, a habitual peck (other than on certain nights) and habitual sleeping positions. She was nineteen.

Jim

He isn't much cop for attending the local races. Instead he listens at his choice of hotel, his loyalty dictated by price and the leniency of the publican as regards credit. From time to time a punter in a suit will call in, fresh from the stands, wafting a sense of occasion. Between races, Ted from Fairlie tells Jim about a motor he's got: not the car itself, just the motor, but it's a finely wrought marvel, well worth the demands it makes and its fits of sputtering temperament. He runs it and tinkers with it and trades parts for it and dreams of putting a body around it.

In this way they fill their ashtray and their afternoon. Fulfil the destiny that can reasonably be expected of them, and lose their money. Jim takes himself off home and wakes the baby coming in, which is punishment enough, but here comes the royal onslaught from the wife. He could undo her arguments, if he could just stand in one place for long enough. When he notices the yellow roses on the kitchen table, he thinks not of his wife's proficiency at growing them but his mother's, because his wife is not coping whereas his mother always did. She reaches something of an ultimatum. Stop drinking so much, she says, or she'll leave him and go south. He's heard it before. His hand closes on a penny in his pocket, and he tries to focus on her tired and fearful expression. She doesn't want to leave.

'How's this,' he says. 'Heads I'll stop, tails I won't. Just like that, no bother or fuss. If it's tails, you do what you need to do. I'll let you go.' She starts crying, as is her wont. He turns his attention to tossing the coin. He hasn't thought past this trick, and only after he catches the coin and slaps it over onto the back of one hand does it occur to him—both ways they both lose. How have they arrived at such abysmal odds? 'Wait a minute,' he says, but his top hand is already drifting up.

He isn't for the island, not yet. They experiment on him first. Send him to a cooling-off place his doctor knows about, a farm in Warkworth run by an Englishman and his wife. Jim doles out slop buckets to the pigs and chickens for a week. Once he's home he visits a Dr Carmichael, who speaks in a repetitive cadence and tells him to relax. He's been here before and the outcome is the same: in the short-term, somnolence; in the long term, hard to say.

He stops at a hotel near Dr Carmichael's surgery afterwards. It's three o'clock on a Tuesday. A smattering of strangers glance at Jim and back to their beers. Here is the publican and here is a jug and here is his glass. Full then empty, then again, until the jug is empty. Here is the publican again, replacing his empty with a full. Jim feels fine now, tip-top, no bother. He's not really drinking, only beer. 'Everyone's a winner when you bring home the beer,' he says. 'It's a winner with dinner.' Publicans are usually good for a yarn or two, early on.

'How's that?' the publican says. He has the same wisp of hair and absence of neck as Jim's neighbour when they were kids.

'It's the advertisement for Coca-Cola, isn't it?' Jim says.

'"The life of the party".'

'That's it.'

'How's your day?'

Jim nods. 'Been to see the doctor.'

'Nothing serious I hope.'

'Not serious, no. More of a joke.'

'Not a very good doctor?'

'Not a very good patient.' Jim opens his hands in a gesture of surrender. 'Better make this the last one,' he says. 'Don't want to be late back.'

'Back to the wife?'

'Back to the wife.' But he isn't so sure. He might need to stop on the way.

'I know this fella,' the publican says. He settles on his stool at the end of the bar and lights a cigarette, one foot on the ground and one on a rung of the stool. 'Liked his beer. When I say I know him, I mean he came in here most days. His wife was a shy little thing, not glamorous, but pretty enough in a dress. Used to come into the lounge bar for a drink on Fridays. Very polite they were; they'd get chatting to people in there, or he would. He had a plumbing business, had a partner and a couple of apprentices working with him. You know, practical common sense type, a few to rub together.'

Jim tries to conjure up the image of a pretty little thing in a dress, after a week of wallowing sows and chicken shit.

'It was always at something like five-thirty that he'd pop through to the public bar and order a beer to drink and a flagon to take home. He'd down his beer, take his flagon out to his car so as not to walk through the lounge bar with it, then he'd go back, collect her, and take her home. My wife and I pieced this together, you see, she serves through there.'

'So one of these Fridays they were in the lounge bar, sitting with another couple, and this bloke excuses himself around half past as usual. But instead of staying at the table like she normally would, the fella's wife takes herself up to the bar and asks my wife for a gin. Nothing with it, mind you—not tonic, not milk, just plain gin.' He grimaced. 'So my wife pours this fella's wife a gin and she pays for it, and she drinks it back right there at the bar.'

'Got himself a handful there.'

'You haven't heard the rest. This girl pulls a face, puts the glass down and says she'll have another one please. "I don't think I can serve you another," my wife says, but hell, it's the first spark the girl's shown all the time she's been coming. "I'll sip it this time," the lass says, "and I'll take some tonic with it and a slice of lemon." Well, she's been sitting on a shandy for the past hour. She's not likely to get plastered on the strength of two gins, so my wife relents. Just a minute.' The publican gets up to pour beers for a customer, puts them down beside the taps on two coasters and flicks the coins into the cash drawer. He leans back onto the stool again. The customer lingers for a moment, but his mate is waiting for his beer.

'So my wife pours the drink,' he continues. 'You know what it's like before closing. Next thing she knows, she's rung the bell, taken last orders and this fella is at the bar asking for his wife. Well. She looks over there and sure enough, the table where they were sitting is empty. The other couple has gone. My wife comes through to me. Have I seen her? No I haven't. My wife checks the bathrooms: not there. "She had a couple of gins," my wife tells him. "Why the hell did you give her those?" "She asked for them." So he went outside to look. Not only was she not there.' The publican leaned forward. '*Nor was his car.* She'd driven off. And not only that, she'd watched and waited until he put the flagon in first. He said he'd never so much as told her where he kept the spare key.'

'Where did she go?'

'Someone saw her parked up in the golf course with one of our other punters drinking the flagon.'

'Jesus,' Jim says. True enough, golf courses are fun places to be drunk, but that's not the point.

'Imagine how that poor bastard felt, having to catch a taxi home and wait for her to bring his car back.' The publican stands up off the stool. 'He still drives it here so she must have got it home in the end. We haven't seen her again.'

'Nothing pretty about a drunk woman,' Jim says.

The publican shakes his head. 'Unless you're drunk yourself, then her face could be on backwards.' He picks up Jim's jug and glass, wipes the bar and puts a fresh towel down, the faded brewery logo that serves as upholstery. 'Another?'

Katherine

A bell tinkled and the door closed behind her. The goods in the shop were arranged by type: overcoats hanging together, radios on one shelf, chests full of tools, and one gesture of display, a stuffed parrot between two pairs of binoculars. A male haunt, down to the aromas of wax and polish, but the proprietor didn't seem surprised to see her. 'Hello Mrs . . .'

'Pardon?'

'Under what name, please?' His sleeves were rolled up. Jowls hung from a pale jaw.

'Oh, I see. Under Brooks, please. Here's the receipt.'

'Jim Brooks gave you this?'

'He's an acquaintance of mine. He's written a note to verify. I was supposed to give it to you with the receipt, sorry.' She placed the sealed envelope on the display glass between them, above a tray of signet rings. On opening it and reading the letter, the broker's frown soon gave way to a chuckle. He was chuckling with Jim, despite Jim being on the island and Katherine standing here in front of him. He folded the paper in half again.

'That will be one pound six, Madam.' She paid him, and he took the note and his knowledge of what the note said with him through the swinging door. A copy of the *Truth* was rolled up beside the cash register.

When he reappeared he put a green metal case on the counter. 'One Singer sewing machine.'

Katherine was irritated. 'I'd like to know your position as regards stolen goods.'

He met her eye for a moment. 'I keep the necessary records. The police come around.' Such men required a precise understanding of their legal rights and obligations.

'If someone brought in a Regency brooch, for example, you would enquire as to whether it had been reported stolen?' The brooch had been left to Katherine by an aunt she had visited in Essex. She was fairly sure she hadn't left it behind anywhere.

'I would report anything suspicious,' he said.

'That's as it should be.'

He rubbed a thick-fingered hand up and down his forearm. 'Do you want the rest of it,' he asked, 'while you're doing Mr Brooks a favour?'

'What do you mean, the rest of it?'

'I'm holding two boxes under his name. He hasn't gone into details here about what you arranged.'

'He only gave me one receipt.'

'Be a shame to see it all auctioned. None of the items are very dear.' The appeal to her good nature didn't suit him.

The bell went again. 'Excuse me for a moment,' he said, all politeness.

Katherine made way for the young man behind her and turned to face the window. Outside, a mongrel sniffed at a lamp post and was tugged away by its neck. A furniture showroom sprawled out on the other side of the road announcing its *WAREHOUSE PRICES!* This was the kind of street one visited for a purpose and left again, not an obvious choice for dog-walking or window-shopping. 'No batteries?' the broker said behind her. A drawer was pulled open and closed, another opened. Eventually a transistor came on and dialled in and out of static, voices and music, before tuning in to one station. The volume went up and down. *It's a WONDERful, protein-ful cereal.* 'Driver's licence please.'

The bell made its tinkling ring again and the door clicked closed. Before Katherine could stop him the broker said, 'Wait there,' and batted one of his saloon doors open. He came back with a cardboard box. The neck of a guitar and at least one picture frame poked out the top.

'Look—' Katherine said. Out he went again. She couldn't help glancing into the box at an album of clear plastic sleeves, the likes of which she had seen before. A few of the coins were set in cardboard and cellophane and labelled, but most were loose in their display pockets, not even polished. A number of the pockets were empty. The collection couldn't have been worth a thing, not in monetary terms. 'Good lord, whose is that,' she murmured.

Down went another box beside the first. 'Two pounds for the lot,' the broker said, rubbing a forearm.

'How long has he got to pay?' she asked.

'You're not going to take it, are you?'

'No I'm not, but thank you for your help.'

'All right.' He yanked the box nearest to him around to pick it up. The sewing machine was quite heavy, and this time the bell seemed to say good riddance.

★

Jim's wife and children lived in a new housing development in Glen Eden: weatherboard and lawn broken up by the odd flowerbed, glimpses of back sections where sheets flapped on clotheslines. Ne'er a tree to be seen. On a hillside behind, the newest houses crouched on their quarter acre of exposed earth. The men had made their morning exodus and left only women and children behind, save the builders who were nailing up the frame of a house on the corner of the Brooks's street. When Katherine pulled up in front of the right letterbox, a boy riding his bicycle on the footpath slowed and put a foot down. He watched her get out of the car, open the back door and pick up the green case. Hers was the only car on the street. Driving in a strange suburb had required all of her concentration.

'Good afternoon,' she said to the boy. Two girls were sitting on the front step of the house opposite dressed up to go out, perhaps ordered to stay put for fear of getting their dresses dirty.

'My mum had one like that,' the boy said. His shorts puffed out from skinny legs. Katherine had encountered a similar directness of manner quite recently, and it might not be a coincidence.

'Do you live here?'

'Yes.' The rapping of the builders' hammers carried over to them.

'In that case, this is your mother's sewing machine.'

'Did you borrow it?'

'As a matter of fact I don't sew.' She realised her mistake.

'Why have you got Mum's sewing machine?'

'Excuse me, I'd better give this to her.' He got off his bicycle, followed her to the door and waited while she knocked. A cat's paw print was set into the concrete on the top step beside his foot.

Mrs Brooks appeared to be respectable despite being young, the wife of an alcoholic and the mother of this private eye, and even if her blouse was half tugged out of her skirt by the infant on her hip. Her small face gave off a hint of impatience. 'Hello,' she said. Her blank look told Katherine that Jim hadn't written any letter.

'Good afternoon. My name is Katherine Morton. I am a journalist writing an article on the Rotoroa Island home, and I've been spending time among the patients there.' Katherine wouldn't have detected any pretence in Mrs Brooks had she not seen the change when she uttered the word 'Rotoroa'. Instant, lived-in concern.

'Including Jim.'

'Yes.'

'You'd better come in.'

In the lounge room Mrs Brooks lowered the baby into a playpen. 'Sit down.' They had a three-piece suite but the walls were bare. The boy leaned one-leggedly on his mother's seat. 'You haven't tried your truck in the sandpit yet, have you?' she said. 'Go on, take it out.'

'Will you come?' he asked. Through the window a web stretching between the leaves of a camellia bush quivered and disappeared in the sunshine.

'We'll see.' He remembered his plans for the truck and ran without looking back. Katherine wondered if she might work in a mention of tea somehow. She had been in her car for the best part of the day, it seemed, and she had to get home yet.

'Where are your family from?' she asked.

'Down south, Otago,' Mrs Brooks said.

'Very beautiful part of the country, especially Queenstown.' Katherine hadn't been to Queenstown in years. 'I always think that kind of beauty lifts us above our own suffering.'

Mrs Brooks seemed unsure how to respond.

'Would you like a cup of tea?' she asked.

'I will if you will.'

Katherine watched the baby bend down—a series of unsteady shifts in her weight—and pick up a wooden block, the G. She met Katherine's eye, victorious, and dropped it over the frame onto the floor outside her pen. The A followed, then T. G, A, T, Katherine thought. Gather your troops.

'What are you doing, silly?' Mrs Brooks put a tray down on an occasional table. She scooped up the blocks and scattered them behind the baby, who wheeled around to where they had landed, dropping onto her bottom. 'Please excuse the house,' she said. There was no mess, only a lack of décor that gave the impression they occupied the house temporarily. 'I've heard of you. Do you still write for the *Herald*?'

'Occasionally, and I've written books, but people often remember me from the children's page "Boys and Girls".'

Not Mrs Brooks, apparently. She unloaded the teacups from the tray.

'I suppose children that age would be listening to jive music now,' Katherine said. It wasn't called jive, was it? Never mind.

Mrs Brooks stood the tray on its side next to her chair.

'You're not going to put us in the paper are you?'

'I'm thinking of writing the article as a kind of ramble around the island, using first names only. I won't include photographs of men who have families, and I always ask permission.'

Mrs Brooks tested the tea in her own cup and poured one for Katherine. She moved the milk jug in Katherine's direction. 'I'm so grateful you brought my sewing machine back.'

'Your husband told me you're a keen seamstress.'

'I've thought of trying to sell things in shops, like aprons and tea cosies. You can make them look quite professional with the right fabric.' The same fabric anyone could acquire if they felt the need to, Katherine assumed. Buttons and hems were her limit, but she was hardly representative. 'Was it in a pawn shop?' Mrs Brooks asked.

Katherine took a sip of scalding tea. Too soon. 'Yes.'

'Do you mind telling me where?'

'In Grey Lynn,' Katherine said. 'I can look up the name.' They must have a phone book, at least.

'Did he give you the money?'

'Yes.' He hadn't. Katherine put her cup back down.

'He was losing on the horses,' Mrs Brooks said.

'So I understand,' Katherine said. Then, hurriedly, 'The camellias grow quickly, don't they?'

'We didn't plant them. The couple before us had to sell up quick. Jim arranged it.'

Katherine regathered her wits. She wasn't there to meddle in their financial affairs. 'I understand Jim attends the Alcoholics Anonymous meetings,' she said.

'Mum!' The boy came rushing in and stopped when he remembered the guest. 'Can I please have a drink?' he said.

'Come on then,' Mrs Brooks said. 'Excuse me.' The boy kept up a breathless commentary as he followed her into the kitchen. He'd chased a dog away from the sandpit and the sand was wet. 'Go and wash your hands,' Katherine heard. 'And stay away from there now.'

'But no!'

'But yes, or I'm coming with you to watch.' Katherine replaced her cup in its saucer more violently than she intended. The baby stared at her, drooling over the corner of an M.

'Sorry,' Mrs Brooks was back again. 'I'll have to shovel that sand out. Bloody dogs. 'Scuse the language. Will you have some more?'

'Please.' Now the boy had shut himself in his room when he should be outside. She wondered how much time the baby spent in her enclosure.

'Sorry, you were talking about Jim going to meetings.'

'Yes, and I must say, he doesn't seem to be in quite the same league as some of the other men, if that's any comfort.'

'What do you mean, the same league?'

'He's more like an average man on the street, less severely affected.'

'Less affected,' Mrs Brooks said.

'And he's trying to make amends now,' Katherine said. 'He must be looking forward to coming home.' Mrs Brooks only looked worried and studied her tea leaves. 'You must be looking forward to having him back. To support you? He won't be drinking,' Katherine said.

'I don't know if he will or not,' the girl replied. She seemed in danger of feeling sorry for herself.

'I understand that men sometimes drink when there are problems in the marriage,' Katherine said.

'I've tried to be patient.'

With relief, Katherine remembered the pamphlet Claire had given her. 'Now listen,' she said. 'Mrs McCallum, the superintendent's wife, told me about these groups.' She opened her handbag, got the pamphlet out and handed it to Mrs Brooks. 'The wives hold their own meetings about what they should and shouldn't do, how they can help. You'd meet other women who understand. A lot of it is getting your emotions under control.' Not that Mrs Brooks had demonstrated much emotion.

'Thanks, that's kind.'

'If you don't mind my asking,' Katherine said. 'How did Jim come to be on the island?'

Mrs Brooks was quiet for such a long time that Katherine went from watching her expression to wondering what she would prepare herself for dinner. The builders' hammers had stopped. 'I'm sorry to intrude,' Katherine said. 'You don't have to answer that.' She thought she ought to be encouraging. 'God has plans for us all. I could attend a meeting with you, if you like.' Mrs Brooks looked up from her tea, not at her visitor but at the unadorned wall.

'I knew Jim had secrets,' she finally said, 'but when the time came, I couldn't face them. He'd gone to put a bet on one Saturday and this boy—an older boy, you know, a teenager—he knocks on the door. I thought he must be a new paperboy, or he'd kicked a ball on the roof. Nice enough boy. But he wanted Jim. I told him Jim was out and asked if I could help. He asked when Jim would be back. "Are you sure I can't help?" I said. "Do you know Jim?" He looked behind me into the house. He seemed a bit agitated. I said that seeing as Jim wasn't home, he had better go. He asked if he could see a photo of him.'

The baby was saying 'Ma-ma-ma'. Mrs Brooks put a rusk from the tea tray into the baby's chubby grip.

'I just wanted to have a normal life. I told the boy to wait and I went inside. In the album I found a photo of my family taken down south a few Christmases ago. Jim hadn't come. Christmas and Jim don't go together very well. I took this photo back and showed it to the boy. I pointed to my brother. That was him, I said. He asked was Jim from Invercargill and I lied. I said he was from Christchurch. He asked had he been married before. I said if there wasn't anything else, could he please go. He gave me the photo back, said sorry, picked up his bike and left.'

'Best not to let your imagination run away with you,' Katherine said.

'Jim had lied to me before, all the time,' Mrs Brooks said, 'but this was different. I was jealous. Isn't that pathetic, of some girlfriend he'd had before me?'

'How old was he when you got married?'

'Old enough. Anyway, after that I went to the doctor about having him committed.'

'It was you?' Katherine was stunned. Judging from her appearance, Mrs Brooks was just another housewife in her twenties, in the hairstyle and attire common to the less affluent tens of thousands, hundreds of thousands, millions like her. Appearance counted for so little.

'I needed two doctors to testify to the magistrate. I went to our doctor first. I told him about the fights me and Jim had, but he said that wouldn't be enough. I told him Jim was taking our things to be pawned, but he said because our possessions were shared by law it wasn't stealing, so finally I told him what I'd found in the cupboard. One day they were there in a box and a few days later they were gone. He told me to go to the police.'

The closer Katherine looked, the more she noticed signs of psychological wear and tear. Since she had begun talking, Mrs Brooks had been pinching a piece of skin on her collarbone repeatedly between her thumb and forefinger. The skin there had become red. 'They gave him his summons without telling him I was involved. When he left the house in his suit that day he said he was going to see about a job.'

A person could be waiting for the right reason, Katherine marvelled, and it could quite literally show up at their front door. She had no doubt in her mind that the boy had been sent to save them that day. 'In this poem I've always liked by Tennyson,' she said, 'the protagonist goes on a quest to avenge his father's death. He travels far and wide, to all these different islands, some of them magic, some of them dangerous, he comes through any number of adventures and trials, and by the time he stands in front of his enemy, face to face, sword in hand, he finds that he has forgiven him.'

Mrs Brooks gave no indication of having understood. Katherine could only press home her point. 'Forgive one another, the Bible says, as God has forgiven you.'

'Who have you had to forgive?' Mrs Brooks asked.

'I had to forgive God for taking my brother. He died at Gallipoli when I was something like your age.'

Mrs Brooks stopped pinching her neck and rubbed the skin to redistribute the blood. 'I'm sorry to hear that, but it's a gutless kind of love God expects, isn't it? He doles out punishment left and right and we're expected to turn to Him for comfort?'

Katherine could only feel sorry for her. Such bitterness. 'I would have been unhappy if I hadn't.'

Something caught her eye in the doorframe, a hand snatching back a blue toy car. 'Your daughter here is lucky'—she waited for Mrs Brooks to look up, and pointed towards the doorway—'to have an older brother to look after her.'

'Derek, are you out there?' Silence from the empty doorframe. 'Come in and sit with Mum.' He waited a few moments, then they heard his limbs shift on the carpet. When he appeared, he didn't quite achieve an amble; he was too obviously aiming for his mother, and too obviously keen to get there. He pulled himself onto the sofa beside her. In contrast to the rest of the surroundings, the suite was rather plush, grey cotton, the print quite modern.

'I didn't finish telling you,' Katherine said. 'I have more of your things in the car to give back. You might be interested, Derek. I don't suppose you collect coins, do you?'

He whipped around to face his mother, and back to Katherine. 'Where did you find them?' he asked. Katherine wasn't going to answer that.

Jim

No bones about it, Captain Mac's office was a good advertisement for clean living. He could see the weather, see if the dinghy was out in the bay, see anyone approaching along the track, watch them coming and going from the workshops. Had the lilies been taken up and planted on the north-facing slope yet? No they hadn't, because there they still were, lined up waiting. But the captain was facing away from the window at present. He preferred to conduct the one-on-ones without distractions and out from behind his desk. They were conversations, not interrogations.

'I don't think I belong here,' Jim said. 'I watched someone try to eat his breakfast with two knives this morning.'

'Would you prefer prison?' Captain Mac asked.

Jim didn't reply.

'There are men don't fit easily anywhere: Mount Eden, Kingseat or here.'

'Does anyone fit in prison?' Jim asked.

'Some cope better than others.' Captain Mac leaned back in his chair, started again. 'How's our garden looking?'

'Not too bad. I didn't get any shells down.'

'You spoke to Miss Morton, did you?'

'Listened, more like.'

'She's been coming here for thirty years.'

'Hasn't she got anything better to do?'

'She's done her fair share.'

'Toff, isn't she?'

The captain paused again and rubbed his chin with a finger. Jim picked up that he was being handled. The thing was, some people were just too cheerful. They had to have the stark reality of a situation pointed out to them.

'What time is your hearing tomorrow?' the captain said.

'Ten o'clock.'

'You know that you're unlikely to be released after the first six months, don't you?'

A shade darker on the other side of the curtains at wake-up call that morning, a shade cooler on the other side of the blanket. Autumn was on its way. 'Would it help if I went to chapel?'

'It's bound to help you personally, yes, but the committee considers things a bit more carefully than that. If you imagine a continuum, Jim, at one end would be the extreme patients—the men you mentioned, for example—who have so many different problems that they'll probably need some form of medical help and supervision for the rest of their lives. At the other end are the ones who succeed in staying sober permanently. You might have heard alcoholics talk about having epiphanies. One day they decide they're going to stop, and they do. Of course, I see God's hand in this.'

What was it about the way they spoke those phrases, 'the Lord', 'Jesus Christ', 'God bless'? They sounded hospitable, but also off-key.

'For the rest, the majority, it takes a few tries and several years. The point is, people can change.'

Jim didn't respond.

'How are relations between you and your wife?'

'Relations?'

'Are you in contact? Do you write to her, tell her your thoughts and feelings?'

The captain might have been in a position of authority, but it wasn't the Sallies regalia that stopped Jim from telling him to pull his head in; it was the boxing history and the tattoos.

'Where is Frank on your scale?' Jim said. 'He's done all the right things and he's still here.'

'Some people go on to serve the community, myself included. And it's taken him a long time. He needs extra support.'

'Why, what's his story?'

'You haven't heard?'

'Nothing scandalous. The war, was it?'

'No, he wasn't considered fit to serve.' Captain Mac crossed his legs at the ankles. 'He was already a chronic drinker by then.' They were the same clodhoppers again, on the same carpet used everywhere. 'I suppose you'll hear it eventually anyway.'

Jim wasn't sure he wanted to know, now he'd asked.

'He and a couple of others were on a binge out in the backblocks of Wanganui,' the captain started. 'For three days they drank at a hotel and took bottles back to Frank's hut. So they were all back there on the third night, stumbling drunk, and one of the men, an English roadworker, lies down on the boards and he says to Frank, "Cut my head off." Apparently this was a stunt he pulled. He'd tell people to shoot him, put him out of his misery, this kind of thing. Keep in mind, these men know each other. They're friends, or as much friends as heavy drinkers can be.'

'Jesus.'

'I'd prefer you didn't use that kind of language, Jim. Young Frank went to the woodpile for the axe, came back inside, and did what was asked of him.'

'He cut his head off?'

'Almost clean off.'

Jim felt nauseous, but scraped out. The sunlight picked out every detail of the shelves, the desk, the windowsills. Never had the edges looked sharper or any of it more indifferent. 'He doesn't seem the violent type.'

'As far as I know he hasn't lifted a finger against anyone since, but I wouldn't necessarily know.'

Jim wasn't so sure. He had the feeling most things got back to Captain Mac eventually. 'Have you thought about what you might do when you do leave?'

'For a job, you mean?'

'Where will you live? It's rough, settling back in sober.'

'I'll go home. We'll manage.'

'My daughter and son-in-law sometimes have people to stay with them for a while.'

'We'll manage.'

'Let me ask you this, then. Are you an alcoholic?' The captain held Jim in his unswerving gaze.

'I am if you say I am. I am if my wife says I am. I'll say so if everyone will give it a bloody rest.'

Lorna

Isaac was gathering fistfuls of fresh grass clippings into piles. 'Leave that where it is,' Lorna told him. 'It's good for the lawn. Frank said.' Frank and his mower had just filled the air with a familiar tang. The pungency came from seaweed on the flowerbeds. Isaac looked every bit the island urchin in his singlet and bare feet, with his skin pinkened by the sun. It had taken him all of a day to adjust. At low tide he had hollered his way across the shining expanse of sand at Ladies Bay, but at high tide he was content to sit near Lorna on the drier, softer drifts, scooping and bulldozing. She'd explored further with him than she had alone. He gave her a reason. He'd asked plenty of questions. 'Does the milkman come to the island? Will Mum and Dad come?' He'd talked about them quite a bit. He sprinkled grass back over everything now, including her hands, where she was poking a hole for a Zinnia seedling.

'Bit late for planting, isn't it?'

Lorna sat back on her heels. Claire McCallum had come through the gap in the hedge: a good Samaritan in short-sleeves with Queen Elizabeth II curls. She was early.

'Jack gave them to me.' Lorna got up and took her gloves off. She had meant to be finished before Claire got there.

'Strange thing for him to do. You'll only have them for a week or two. You're helping are you, Isaac?' Claire asked. She said to Lorna, 'I thought I'd listen to the sermon with you.' The Reverend Billy Graham was being broadcast from North Carolina. Some of Lorna's comrades, including the McCallums, were going to hear him preach in his New Zealand crusade.

Inside, Claire pulled a chair out and sat down at the kitchen table. Lorna had already tidied up, thank goodness. 'Nothing for me, no tea,' Claire said. 'What time do you have to be away?'

'Just before ten-thirty,' Lorna said. Paul had been the one to make the doctor's appointments. Lorna had been distracted by the prospect of Isaac coming. She turned the dial to 1YA.

'Here I am!' Isaac had followed them in.

Lorna said, 'You can play quietly in here or outside, but only on the lawn.'

'I think I'll stay put,' Claire said.

'No, me!' Isaac said.

'And what are you going to do then?' she asked.

He rushed out again in case they changed their minds. He was still small enough that he'd have to slow down for the steps and take them one at a time.

'It's all good practice, isn't it?' Claire said. 'Your time will come, you and Paul.'

The New Zealand announcer finished, and the Reverend's voice came through the speakers. 'I'm going to ask that we bow in prayer,' he said. His calling had taken him around the world like a film star, or a knight, sparring with temptation. His intentions would have been less worldly, but his drawl and his seesawing cadence brought the whole sprawling spectacle of America, complete with gigantic cars, space rockets and protest marches, to Lorna's kitchen table. 'Everyone here should know by now that their salvation lies in Jesus Christ,' the Reverend said. 'If they don't, well, I'm here to convince them of it.' He made special appeals to young people. He said they could change the world with their energy and belief. He was too ecumenical, Lorna had heard other people say— older people, she supposed. She thought he sounded different to Neil, but it had been so long since she'd heard Neil's voice that she couldn't remember exactly what he'd sounded like. She stared beyond the radio's grille at the fabric behind. Paul had moved it in from the lounge for her that morning, so she'd be able to listen there, in her territory.

The first she was aware that the sermon was over was when the voices flattened out into the familiar accent, from persuasive to informative. Claire was still writing in the notebook she'd brought with her. 'I liked what he said about some people's consciences being dulled,' she said. 'That could be the men here, couldn't it? They're like the crowd in the parable of the sower: *they may see, and not perceive . . . they may hear, and not understand.*'

'How would someone know if their conscience had been dulled?' Lorna asked.

'They would lose sight of Christ, wouldn't they? They would lose their way and things would go wrong in their lives.'

'But things go wrong for people who do follow Him, too. I mean, from the patients' perspective, how are they supposed to tell the difference?'

Claire's ears were glowing at the edges where the sun lit them from behind. 'We can't always know His will. *Trust in Jehovah with all thy heart, And lean not upon thine own understanding.*' She had a verse for every occasion.

Lorna stared out the window dumbly at the seedlings in their pots, waiting on the edge of the flowerbed. Something was missing.

'You'd better get on, had you?' Claire asked.

'Where's Isaac?' Lorna hadn't seen any blur of movement or heard any sound effects—his *bzh* engine noises or battle cries—for at least a few minutes. She got up. No need to panic, the chances of anything bad happening were so slim, as slim as the odds of winning a sweepstake. 'He must have gone around the front,' she said.

Claire followed her down the steps. The empty lawn, the two ways out, the stray clippings, all declared his absence. She darted around the side of the house to the more shaded front door, which they hardly ever used. Not there, just a neat strip of grass.

'Isaac!'

He didn't answer. He wasn't around the back, either, with the odd lengths of timber and the damaged wringer they'd never found a use for.

'Not there, Lorna?'

'No. I'll go down the track.'

'I'll go up.'

How much distance could he have covered? To get to Ladies Bay he would need to cross to the far end of Home

Bay and choose the correct track, then take the right turn at the fork a hundred yards later. The thought of him on those tracks, such a tiny figure, was wrong, but it was all so improbable, him alone anywhere. Lorna jogged out of the front gate, joined the track, and started down, already drawn to the water. These things happened to people, they did. She ignored the path that split off to the left. If he was getting under someone's feet in the workshops he could stay there for now. She stopped noticing her footfalls. She carried on down until she reached the end of Palm Walk, puffing, and scanned the beach stones, scanned the water. Everything slowed down, made vivid. She couldn't see him. Only a yellow buoy bobbed out there, nothing in a singlet. She could have drifted free from her body, so little was she aware of it.

'Isaac!'

Set some way back from the water, to her left, were the rows of the vegetables. The men working there had seen her and straightened up, but they were much too big. Paul wouldn't be there. He was with the doctor. Would Isaac hide from her? Across the bay, sheep in a paddock munched grass. One or two raised their heads.

If he'd crossed the bay, he would have been distracted by the animals or the workshops. Behind her, on the other side of the track she'd come from, was a stand of pines the children liked. They even had a name for it, the fairy woods. The timber was hardly ever used. Any felling was done during the week, while the children were having their lessons. On days like today. A gnawing tunnelled into Lorna's stomach as she jogged back through the palms. She tried to see into the trees before she got there but her vision played tricks with the overlapping boughs. Isaac must know his fairy tales. To enter the woods was to ask for trouble. She crossed the track and stepped into the shade, onto an undulating carpet of needles that gave off fragrant air, warm and inviting. She would have gone in if she were him. For a moment, there was no sound, just silence, no birdcalls, not even a fly, then she heard men's voices and the thwack of tools. Fear clamped down on her. So this would be it, not the water.

'Wait! Isaac!' She looked for him in the patterns of sunlight. She looked for the men, anyone. 'Dear God,' she thought. 'Please help. Please let him be okay. I promise I'll be more faithful. I promise.'

Of course, she forgot all about that as soon as she heard Claire behind her.

'Lorna, he's here!' The tone of her voice told Lorna to stop panicking, that the world was waiting to welcome her back.

A blue shirt appeared fifty yards ahead of her, breaking up the layers of ash brown and golden light between them.

'You all right?' the man yelled.

Lorna waved at him. 'Fine!' Above, the pine needles were still green.

'There's no one allowed in here today.'

'Sorry!' She couldn't see Isaac yet. She jogged back to Claire, sweating under her blouse, and they started up the track. Jim was further up, near the hedge, holding a wheelbarrow. Isaac was his passenger. His feet stuck out the end and he held on at the sides. He stopped jiggling his legs when he saw Lorna. When she reached them she lifted him out. He squirmed to be let down.

'Where was he?' she asked. Jim's skin was sallower than it should be in late summer, as though he was the one who'd been hiding out in the woods.

'Mai Mai,' Jim said. 'I was there for shells.' So it had been a close call. She could see from the stubborn set of Isaac's mouth that he was trying to hide something. He was frightened. He knew he'd roamed too far. She wanted to bend down and put her arms around him and hold on, but he wouldn't have let her.

'He didn't do any harm,' Jim said. They were an odd pair, the sunburnt boy and the man, but they were a pair somehow; it was Lorna who was interfering.

'That's very naughty, Isaac,' she said. 'I told you to stay in the garden.' Isaac put his head down. 'Say thank you to Jim,' she said.

'Thank you.'

'Be good,' Jim said. 'I'd better get on.' He picked up the handles again. 'Cable Bay this time.' There were hardly any shells in the wheelbarrow's tray, only a bucket's worth.

'Wasn't that where you were headed this morning?' Claire asked.

'I thought I'd try Mai Mai first.'

Claire watched him push off. He took the path to the workshops. 'You go,' she said to Lorna. 'You might still make it.'

The doctor saw patients in a room off the hospital ward. Lorna was still flustered when she arrived, and instead of using the door from the outside, she took the more intrusive route through the ward, where there was a patient sleeping with the curtains pulled—the insularity of a dark room on a sunny day. She surprised the doctor, whose chair was facing the other way. 'Sorry I'm late,' she said. 'We had a problem.' The signs everywhere were standard-issue Salvation Army, green with white lettering, similar to what she'd seen at college.

WASH YOUR HANDS above the sink. Only a few members of staff were allowed in that room unaccompanied. Lorna wasn't one of them.

'I'm sure it couldn't be helped. Take a seat.' Lorna sat in the chair opposite him. When she saw the manila folder open on his lap she felt a familiar tension creep over her. 'Now, for questions regarding fertility, I would usually meet with husband and wife together, but in your case I thought I would speak to you separately first.'

Lorna nodded. She and Paul still hadn't talked properly. He was nervous about fatherhood, but he wasn't the only one with conflicting feelings.

'I would normally enquire about your health, your menstrual cycle and so on,' the doctor said. 'Depending on how you answered, we might do various tests. There are a few potential problems we would look out for.' He crossed one leg over the other. 'However, and I imagine you must know what I'm going to say, much of the investigation we would normally do is unnecessary because you have already carried a child to term.' She found it hard to look at him, but when she did he was serious, not disapproving. 'Can I assume that your husband doesn't know?'

'No, he does.'

He pushed his glasses up on his nose. 'Well, that's good. That's good.' The second time, he said it to himself.

'And the child—a boy it says here—he was adopted?'

'Yes, by my parents.' It was out before she realised that it was irrelevant.

'By your parents?' Lorna couldn't remember a doctor having made sustained eye contact with her before. He looked much the same as anyone else. His hair had been flattened by his hat and in the warm weather it was still partially stuck to his forehead. In different clothes, he could have been a tram conductor or worked in a shop like Grandpa, selling reels of cotton.

'So he's being raised as your . . .'

'As my brother.'

He didn't drop his gaze. His expression didn't betray any reaction. 'That must be hard,' he said. 'For you, that is.'

Lorna studied the bench behind him, the tap, an empty shelf. All of the first-aid supplies were locked away. It half resembled a sickbay.

'I'm sorry,' the doctor said. 'Take your time.'

'No, it's good,' she said, when she could trust her voice. 'I mean, thank you. It has been.' The pent-up feeling gradually eased off, and after a while her breathing returned to normal. 'I don't suppose many of your other patients would be in this situation, would they?'

He frowned slightly, as though he were trying to remember. 'Perhaps not this situation, exactly.'

The glare of high sun had faded by the time Paul joined Lorna and Isaac outside the chapel. This was the only church she'd seen that was clad in corrugated iron. The tin tabernacle, Captain McCallum called it. Inside, the congregation sat bunched up in the small space, and passed down the aisles by twos at the most. Exposed timber beams reminded her of Mr Purcell and the sawyers in the yard with their pies. The savings she'd accumulated while she'd worked there were still sitting in a bank account she never used.

Lorna wished she hadn't agreed to preach a sermon that day of all days. She reminded herself that people were there to hear God's word, that they weren't interested in her, but the longer she waited through the notices and the hymns, the more envious she became of the patients gazing into their laps or at the corps flag, who were able to stay where they were, with nothing more demanded of them than their presence. She found herself staring at the back of Captain McCallum's head in the front row, round and greying, a fold of skin where it met his neck. Everyone appeared to be relaxed, not panicked like she was. Beside her, Isaac fidgeted with the hem of his shorts and put his fingers in his mouth. She pulled his hand down. She had been taught to direct her voice to the back of the room; in this case, to the table of bibles and hymnbooks and the stacks of spare chairs. Quite a bit of her life so far had been spent in rooms with stacks of spare chairs. She had unfolded and folded up heaven only knew how many trestle tables and probably arranged thousands of biscuits on plates.

When Captain Sharpe invited her up, she let her legs carry her along the aisle to the lectern. She looked out to the back of the chapel. Only a couple of the spare chairs were being used that afternoon, one of them by Jim, who she'd never seen at a service before. She might have suspected him of being there to swipe something, if she'd thought there were anything worth taking. She wondered if it was calm in his mind, in the eye of his own storm. He was probably thinking of something or someone completely unrelated to her sermon, or even to God for that matter. It was a relief to think he didn't expect much, him or any of the others. 'I recently reread Matthew twenty-three,' she started.

After she sat down, Captain Sharpe led the blessing. 'Would our men who have served in Egypt, Italy and the Pacific—

correct me if I've missed anyone—please stand.'

A handful of men got to their feet, including Captain McCallum.

'Tom McFarlane,' Captain McCallum said. 'Is he here?'

'Yep, I'm coming,' Tom answered. He was having more difficulty straightening up than the others. With his scant white hair and creaky ways, Tom looked as though he could be someone's grandfather, but he didn't have anyone, so Lorna had been told.

Captain Sharpe stepped down into the aisle and raised his hands, palms open. 'Lord, these men have served their country,' he said. Isaac squirmed between Paul and Lorna. The shirt and clean shoes didn't quite tame his new wildness. Paul patted his knee absentmindedly and Isaac looked up at her, appealing to her to understand his plight, stuck in church while there was daylight outside, but he had done enough exploring for one day.

'Please ease their troubles,' the captain said. The men bowed their heads. 'We pray for them as we ourselves strive to serve and make sacrifices.'

When the men sat down, Claire walked up and stood to one side of the rostrum on one of the steps. 'Which hymn shall we finish with?'

'Seventy-three,' one of the men called out.

'Sixteen,' said another.

'Seventy-three is the easier to play,' Claire said. 'I think Captain Sharpe would thank me for that.' She raised her voice and led them all along. Even Captain Sharpe watched her from the piano. At the increase in activity, Isaac began rocking forwards and backwards in his seat.

'Sit still,' Lorna whispered. 'This is the last one.' Paul

turned around at the sound of her voice, lifted Isaac up and sat him on his lap. Isaac became as still as he had been in the wheelbarrow. When the chorus came, Paul's fingers fluttered the tune against his shin.

Paul still wasn't back when Lorna lit the lamps at half past nine and picked up her Bible. The columns of crammed text, the delicate paper and the lamplight on the page had a cooling effect on her mind. She didn't know what to do with the sense of freedom she had, the relief of the day being over. A morepork called every now and then and, for a few minutes at a time, if Isaac changed position or opened his mouth, the sound of his breathing carried from the room where he was sleeping. She'd left the curtains open to give her a view of moonlight swimming in the bay. Each window's angle was slightly different. Even in the rooms along the front of the main block, each frame would pull in or leave out a tree here or rock there.

She heard Paul's footsteps on the gravel of the track, nothing while he crossed the lawn, then the back door opening. The coal shovel in the bin, and the handle on the range door scraping open and closed. Some days he'd return home and it was as though he'd only left the room and come back, as though she'd lost the entire day, but not today.

He appeared in the doorway. 'Still up?' he asked. He had gone from a school uniform straight into the Salvation Army garb, but since Lorna had seen what was underneath, she'd paid little attention to the clothes. The flesh was what was essential. Their dynamic was different, when they were laid bare.

'What's happened?' she asked. Captain McCallum had called him away after the service. He no longer had his goggles of pale skin, she noticed. She couldn't recall seeing him wearing his glasses at all that day. His eyes were just another feature of him she'd grown accustomed to and took for granted.

'Four of the men got drunk last night on parsnip wine.' He couldn't quite keep the excitement out of his tone.

'You're kidding. Who?'

'Gerald and Jim Brooks. I don't know if you know Don and Phillip? They're off on the next boat.'

'Who caught them?'

'Claire noticed something off about Jim today. They pieced it together from there.'

'But it was Jim who brought Isaac back when he ran off.'

'You didn't tell me Isaac ran off.'

'I hadn't had a chance.'

'He's too small to be off by himself.'

'I'm quite capable of worrying about him myself, thanks.' She couldn't help it.

'He's my worry if he's in my care.' Paul sat down in the armchair opposite. 'I do worry about him. I feel sorry for him.' He was holding something in his hand, a record cover. The picture on the front was of a Negro man in a suit and cap, jammed into a child's trolley. 'Have you thought about whether you'll tell him one day?' As if the problem had only recently occurred to him. As if he wasn't sure whether she would have had the same foresight.

'What do you think, Paul? Of course I have.'

'Steady on.' He was used to all kinds of lip from the patients, but Lorna didn't usually raise her voice to him.

He tried a different subject. 'What are you reading?'

'The rest of Matthew. *For ye are like unto whited sepulchres, which outwardly appear beautiful, but inwardly are full of dead men's bones, and of all uncleanness.*' With effort, she pulled herself back. 'How was the doctor?'

'We have to wait for my results, but he said to keep trying in the meantime.' He smiled. His dimples were youthful, but youth in him didn't necessarily have positive associations. He had been tapping different edges of the record cover against his knee, doing quarter turns, since they'd been sitting there.

'What's that?'

He turned the cover over to look at. 'Jim gave it to me. Told me to keep it.'

'Are you allowed to accept it?'

'I'll have to ask.'

The phone rang, but it wasn't their code and they ignored it.

'Put it on,' she said.

'What about Isaac?'

'He won't wake up. Go on.' Lorna stood up to close the door to Isaac's room. When she got back Paul was bent over the record player. Two or three horns started to play together, plodding, with no subtlety or variation. Each phrase ended abruptly.

'Is that "Abide With Me"? What are they trying to do?'

'I think it will change,' he said. 'I think he's having us on.'

He was right. A piano came in, then a rhythm section and the brass, and Paul and Lorna were quiet for a while. The piano led at first, snatches of unpredictable notes to hold the attention. A saxophone joined in. They broke off and went their own ways, then reordered themselves. It was less like listening to music than adjusting to a new environment, like having company.

'We had Coleman Hawkins recordings at school,' Paul said eventually. 'I used to want to go to New York and see some of these players.'

'So did I.' Lorna nodded her head on the beat. 'I mean, not to hear these players, but I wanted to go to America.' The shyness she felt must stem from how far back this went, back to before she'd learned how unlikely it was. Making another human being had turned out to be easier: too easy, and too difficult.

Paul didn't say anything for the length of the trumpet solo. When the double bass took its turn, he sat down opposite her again. 'So who was the Mormon?' he asked.

She might never have said his name aloud, she realised. To her parents, he was Elder Cowley.

'Neil,' she said.

Paul pinched his chin. The drummer was bashing away now, deafeningly. 'What happened?'

It didn't seem the right time to ask him to turn the volume down, so she tried to concentrate. 'I had a crush on him. I thought he wanted to marry me.'

'It wasn't that bloke at the dance, was it?'

'Alan? Is that what you thought?'

'Mormons might dance. I didn't know. You like listening to rock and roll, don't you?' Crash, crash, went the drums. It was almost painful.

'I suppose so.'

The drums finally faded back, but the rhythm was still frenetic enough to jump her nerves. Paul tapped his feet. 'I'd ask you for a clandestine dance, if I could think of a way to dance to this.' She laughed. 'We could use it for a scripture march,' he said.

The brass blared back in loud again, and they almost missed the phone.

Two long and two short, two long and two short, two long and two short—it was their ring this time. 'Shall I?' he asked. He got up and lifted the needle off the record.

Lorna could just see the tops of the first pair of phoenix palms, the first of a parade. No parade of trees would help a down-and-out drunk, not really.

'Lorna.' She didn't answer him at first. 'Lorna!' She looked up. 'It's your dad,' he said. 'It's about your mum.'

Jim

For a long time there are working days between drinks: entire mornings and afternoons, at least. But after the furniture shop there are only a few hours after waking up. His credit dries up at the local hotel. The missus drops the kids with a girl she knows in the neighbourhood and goes to work at the switchboard. Rain or shine, hell or high water, he has a shave and goes out for his paper and flagons.

It's 'Morning, Jim' at the dairy. On the front page here's another one of your mushroom clouds over an atoll, stacked up beside the sixpenny mixtures with the tops of the bags twisted into ears. Some days he stops in at the TAB to collect. On Fridays he picks up a pencil and a fresh ticket and opens the guide from under his arm. He checks the tote. A shilling each way and if he's feeling lucky a double. Behind her machine at the counter she reads his selections back to him: some days he bets on two races, some days four and some days all eight. She has a bit of meat on her bones but he doesn't mind that. 'Think I'll get lucky today?' he says. She doesn't know he isn't on his lunch break or in charge of his own business, and what she doesn't know can't hurt his chances.

'Good luck, Sir,' she says. The same thing to every customer, every time. Her boss is watching, after all. They know him at the bottle shop. Three of DB Draught please, and put the empties on the counter, fewer words exchanged the better. He watches the last drops of foam fall into the drip tray as the flagon's pulled away; this part isn't auspicious but it's necessary. Can't say he hasn't got good use out of these flagons. They're heavy to carry home. At first he waits until after lunch to pour his first glass, then it's eleven o'clock, then ten. He switches the wireless on and arranges his beer, his ashtray, his pen and his newspapers on the side table.

For the first few glasses on a Saturday he's busy, noting down the results and, between races, making his picks for the next meetings. He can call up a mental image for the best-known breeders, trainers and jockeys. The big families of the sport—your Pooles, your Marshalls and your Doyles—up and down he follows their fortunes. His wife grew up among horses but she couldn't care less.

By the time she dumps the baby in her highchair for her lunch he's reading the paper. A 'Cash for Stamps' advert has captured his attention, even through the early glow off the beer. While he's thinking it over, the boy approaches with his latest shanghai. In some moods Jim takes him out the back to use it. The missus yells to them from the clothesline to be careful, to aim into the empty section. Jim points it at her, a dummy target, and the boy laughs, and she laughs a laugh that's convincing enough. When she goes inside he and the boy might aim for next door's cat, and they might hit it, but they're only using clods of dried-up dirt most of the time, which only send it streaking over the fence and out of range.

When he's tired of that, he'll plot a course back to the kitchen to refill his beer. En route he'll break the baby out. She'll be lying there, helpless, like a beetle flipped onto its back, struggling to focus on the object dangling over her, a tizzied-up clothespeg or similar piece of fuss. He'll be amazed at her persistence, at how many times she'll reach out to grab it and fail. Then he'll lift her, and in a flash it's gone. She hardly reacts at all, unless to be stupefied is a reaction. Once he has her, he might surprise her with a feat of disappearance and reappearance, or offer up his finger as bait, let her catch it occasionally. Then he'll remember his abandoned glass. 'I'll have her in the highchair, please,' the missus says.

The baby used to eat her tea with the rest of the family, but eventually that show went from being entertaining to frustrating to downright bloody irritating, the way she'd smeared her food on the highchair and herself, dumped it on the floor—then leaned to the side to see where it landed. Now the missus feeds her first and the three of them sit up afterwards. The boy is to eat everything that's dished up to him, regardless of quality. As an adult, he'll have earned the right to complain but by hell he'd better not try it under Jim's eye. He'll eat his cauliflower. He'll eat his peas. What happened to the pork roast Jim brought home for the freezer? They ate it at Easter, she'll remind him, and he'll recall that the cousins left immediately after dinner and that will rile him.

After dinner she ushers the children off, which is fine by Jim—they're grating after a while. Now he can settle in. The wireless goes on. He drifts. The second empty flagon goes in the wash-house and he twists the top off a new one.

Back in the lounge he uses his pencil to tap the objects within reach: his glass, the corner of the table, the side of the ashtray, a plastic trinket the boy left behind, a kind of dome with a castle inside. You tip it wrong-side up and flakes of something inside fall like snow. He's a conductor warming up the orchestra. He's got no money to go out, so he drinks on, pouring in enough for a mist to settle into his skull. It's very important that nobody should disturb this. He might take himself off to the shed to strip the paint off that stool. He may or may not get himself back in, or he might reach halfway in and have a rest on the lounge floor that lasts all night. If he makes it all the way he'll probably slide a couple of records out of their sleeves (the player has survived thus far) and turn up the dial. He might do any number of things. In some respects it hardly matters because he probably won't remember, but there's usually an altercation before he goes down—a last hurrah.

Katherine

'Congratulations are in order I hear. Your Sunday Island book—going from strength to strength.' Richard sat leaning his prominent chest forwards, which made his legs seem short.

'The Star in Johannesburg is going to serialise it,' Katherine said. 'That makes three.' The *Times* of London hadn't wanted it. One could always have done better. Richard wasn't English as many of the previous editors had been, but he had a miniature bust of the Bard pinning down letters on his desk. Katherine had already been a veteran when he'd started as a mid-tier journalist twenty years ago. She didn't envy him his role keeping everyone happy—the paper's owners, its readers, scores of journalists and the police and politicians. They waited for his secretary to unload a tray of coffee and cake. The office didn't look out over a newsroom exactly, the building was too labyrinthine for that, but it did have a large window onto the corridor, and the backs of a few typists and telephonists across the way: the rooms with the greatest concentration of women.

'Are you still enjoying working independently?' he asked.

'The baking isn't as good,' she said. She took a moist forkful of lemon cake. 'This is delicious.' Female readers had sent her tin after tin of Louise cake, shortbread and the rest, perhaps hoping she would publish the poems their children had written.

'Shirley baked. It's my birthday.'

'Richard! I wish you'd told me.'

'Why? We're inundated already. I watched one of the court reporters wrap up an entire cake and put it in his briefcase earlier.' He swallowed his last mouthful, sipped his coffee and retrieved his cigarette from where it was smoking gently in the ashtray. 'None of them eat breakfast.'

'Well, happy birthday. What's news?'

'We're putting together a special for the bridge opening. Holland and Nash have both written proud christening speeches.' They would all have invitations to the ceremony and be caught up in the excitement. 'How were they on Rotoroa?'

'That's why I came in. I've had an idea about a new approach I'd like to try.'

'I'm surprised you felt you needed to come in. We trust you.'

'The tone of my visit was different this time, somewhat more personal.'

'They're doing new things over there, aren't they?' he said. 'It's only fitting to reflect that in the writing.' She could tell he was curious by the way he sat back, waiting to hear.

'I thought you really hit on something with the style of the Sunday Island book, the balance of documentary and drama.'

'I spoke to one patient in particular who put me in contact with his wife here in Auckland.'

'And she helped you fill in the background?'

'She did.'

'So long as we include the usual facts and figures, by all means let's hear about this patient. What's his name?'

'Jim.'

'First names only, of course.' Richard crushed out his cigarette.

It occurred to Katherine that after putting out a cigarette he would usually stand and offer her a jolly farewell. 'Sorry,' she said. 'I'm not explaining this very well.' She found herself speeding up. 'The superintendent, Captain McCallum, spends a lot of time with the patients, and less time on his administrative duties than the others did. That is, he spent less time with me.' Must be the coffee making her jumpy. She didn't drink it very often.

Richard frowned. 'They didn't palm you off, did they? Do you need me to write any letters on your behalf?'

'No, nothing like that. Claire gave me everything.'

'Claire?'

'Captain McCallum's wife. She helps with the accounts and running the office.' She stretched the pins and needles out of her hand.

'Good on her. I'm sure he needs all the help he can get.'

'I'm sorry. I'm getting to this by a rather tortuous route.'

'Not at all.' He reached out for his cigarette packet.

———

London, 1939. Katherine's neighbour had found her crying in their shared hallway and invited her in. They were in West Kensington and the building's tenants were respectable, but this being London and space being at a premium, the rooms were all-in-one. Like Katherine's, her neighbour's hob was in her living area, which was itself one side of the bedroom. She had a vase of hyacinths on the deep window ledge. Their perfume was strange to Katherine and unusually pervasive. 'I'm sorry to impose like this,' she said. 'You caught me at one of those moments.'

She had spent the day being rejected by bespectacled young editors on Fleet Street, which was all the more galling considering the time she'd spent sending her portfolios ahead, making appointments, planning and rehearsing her routes and reading that morning's editions before setting out, and how thrilled she'd been to find it much as she had imagined: the familiar names of the papers, narrow buildings jumbled in, billboards, the dome of St Paul's at one end. Afterwards she had limped home through the drizzling indifference of an autumn evening, brick and concrete and cobblestones, with a blister on her heel, to see an overdue rent notice slipped under her door.

The neighbour was a country rose type with round eyes, rouged cheeks and fading hair that really ought to have been worn shorter. She was a teacher, describing herself as a school mistress. Unlike most of the tenants she seemed to live there permanently. At home, people might have been tempted to ask questions about a woman in her situation. 'I would have been terrified,' she said. 'Who did you meet with?'

'Several people. The travel editor from the *Daily Telegraph* said a good proportion of their readers were likely to be familiar with the countries I've visited and would expect deeper analysis of the political or cultural context,' Katherine had told her. She would never have said all of this to such a fleeting acquaintance in New Zealand.

'You must have travelled a great deal.'

'The *Illustrated London News* called my style romantic. He said they have a vicar in the Home Counties who writes for them from a spiritual perspective occasionally.'

The neighbour had blinked her round eyes. 'My brother is a vicar,' she'd said, 'but he's quite cynical.'

Katherine had felt as though she was drawing the fragrance of the hyacinths in through her pores as well as her lungs, being saturated by it. 'I would have thought people would welcome spiritual comfort in anxious times,' she'd said. 'It's not that I haven't reported on the grittier subjects, but I feel compelled to offer hope or consolation.'

The neighbour had pulled her legs up onto the armchair and tucked them under her body. 'The papers don't tend to concern themselves much with people's spiritual welfare. They should, possibly.' She didn't appear to have anywhere else to go or anything else to do. 'Would you like a glass of sherry?'

'I'd better not,' Katherine said. No good would come of dissipation. Despite her having been brought low, life went on outside the window. It had begun to rain silently. Passersby below them paused under street lamps and disappeared beneath the ink blots of their umbrellas. She had begun to find the scent of the flowers vaguely rank. Whenever she shared confidences she came away feeling depleted, as though she had been hoodwinked. She and the teacher hadn't known each other for long, so why confide, and why listen?

Life had gone on. Hollingworth had got the scoop in Poland. Katherine had recovered from her disappointment that day and years later had become curious about how her neighbour had fared during the war, whether she'd remained in London or gone home, wherever home was: perhaps a village green and country lanes that tunnelled through overhanging boughs.

'I'd like to write about the women: the wives of the alcoholics, the wives of the staff on the island, their experiences.'

'Their experiences?'

'Yes. Imagine trying to raise two children by yourself. Imagine keeping house with hardly any clean water and having to work by candlelight, cook on an iron range and scrub your clothes in a copper, in this day and age!'

'But the Rotoroa home is for men—for men and staffed by men.'

She had a dead feeling in her arm now, and a headache coming on, really quite sore, but she was determined to get her point across. 'The women have more insight. They were sober, you see, the wives. They were in a better position to observe. The men were drunk.'

'We're getting a bit off-topic,' Richard said. 'We have an arrangement with the Ministry of Justice regarding Rotoroa. They invite us there, invite you there, and we update the public on the good work they do.'

'Don't we also represent the interests of the patients and their families, and the wider good?' Some of her words were running together as though she were the one drinking. It was embarrassing.

'Most of the men don't have any families, do they?'

Richard held an unlit cigarette between his fingers. 'But of course we do. And that's why you're just the person to cover Rotoroa.' He gestured to someone behind her, outside the window, half acknowledgement, half dismissal (it was enough to make Katherine lose her train of thought). 'You must know they were taking a lot of flak before McCallum came in, threats of closure, even. The new Wellington programme is in the inner city, where there's better access.' He conjured a flame and held it up to the cigarette between his lips. 'How would this be: you write your state-of-the-nation report, the kind we usually do, with the new buildings, new boat, new superintendent and so on. For the other . . .' he sat forward. 'We've got a new page launching next month, "Women's World". I'll put you on to the editor. Most of the writing will be light-hearted, but I can't imagine she'd turn down a chance to have something from you.'

This made sense, but only if Katherine used every ounce of her concentration.

'If the timing is off and she can't place it, the *Woman's Weekly* will take you in a flash.'

She could hardly lift her left arm. And there was another problem. She couldn't see Richard very well. She began to feel apprehensive.

'I can't—' was what she said, but it came out 'I carm'.

'Katherine?' Richard's purposeful cheer vanished and his expression became grave. That in itself was more alarming than anything else.

Jim

The notes of the piano jarred, the last of the day's gulls cried overhead. The young lass got up and hid her stiff shoulders behind the pulpit. She stared at the back wall, then directly at Jim, then at her paper. 'I recently reread Matthew twenty-three,' her reedy voice said. 'This is verse twelve: *Be not called Rabbi, for one is your Master and all of you are brothers.* What does this mean? It means none of us should come to believe that we have all the answers. *Call no man your father upon the earth. One is your Father, which is in heaven.'*

'You men complain that your letters are checked before they reach the mail sack. It might help you to know that my husband read my sermon before tonight's service. I remind myself that his work is supervised by Captain McCallum and the Captain's by the territorial command and the Justice Department.' Shifting in seats and a clearing of the throat.

'We can all benefit from others' experience.'

'Christ died and he returned so we could learn from his experience. In this, I believe he acted as both your brother and advisor. For you men have undergone a kind of death, every time you reached for a drink. You died when you gave your souls to addiction.' She was out of the gate now, off and running. 'You are here for no other reason but to be brought back to life. Christ needed God to give him back life and we need God to bring us back. We don't have this power ourselves. Now you might say that Christ did not die and rise, die and rise, and die again several times, as some of you appear to have done.' A laugh for that. 'Here is my answer to that: until the day when you refrain from drinking alcohol for good, you are still as if dead. You have not been given a new life because *you have not asked for one.* You are grappling with your old life and your old master. Let them go. Accept God, and you will live again.'

★

They have regulation candles stuck to regulation saucers. The flames scatter their wavering glow across the men's faces. The wine, far from regulation, isn't what Jim was expecting. The faint parsnip flavour is sweet, not unpleasant. They drink fast, keeping pace. Months are being undone in moments: the thought carries unease and leaves some to linger when it departs. The syrupiness of this new tipple is new but the come-on of intoxication—and it comes on quickly—is a homecoming. In the warm flush of reunion Jim puts his mug down and gets to his feet, not as steady as he intended. 'Any of you heard the one about the pope and the octopus?' he says.

'Sit down.'

They'll keep. He lands heavily in his chair.

'When's Hendry going to get his wife up the duff? A shilling says she won't fit into her jacket by the end of the year.'

'I'll take that bet.'

'You don't reckon Miles Davis is giving it to her?'

'Something's not right.'

'We might get kicked out before that.' But they're all used to tuning out reality as though it's radio static, that's the point of the exercise. Here is where they stop being individuals with pasts and problems, and cross over into grouphood, here and now and parsnip wine. For as long as they're drinking they can stay in this dimension. Jim lifts back the curtain beside him. Frank is bent over on the path outside. No, not on the path, in the flowerbed. A full moon picks out the white roses and beyond that the whitewashed steps leading up to the chapel. 'What are you doing?'

'Frank is taking the heads off the roses out there,' he says. 'Should we be worried?'

'Nah, his hearing's shot.'

'But why is he?'

'Why not? Probably can't sleep.'

It was Gerald who'd made the wine and buried the flasks a few metres off the track on Pakatoa Point. He'd uprooted a gorse bush to plant on top. When Jim offered to put a seat in amongst the scrub near the point—clear a patch facing out towards the view—Gerald was forced to let him in on the secret. He got paranoid. He began to see the stash as a liability. He dreamed one night that he was with one of the lieutenants when they heard a deep hum coming from just that spot. In the dream he pretended not to notice. *It's coming from under the gorse bush*, the dream lieutenant said. *I've never understood why this gorse bush is here.* Gerald excavated his wine first in dreams (in which he uncovered all manner of malignancies) and then, in reality, by scrambling out of the window, retrieving a spade he'd stashed amongst the pilings that supported the water tank, and hefting, rolling, dragging the flasks back to secrete them amongst the same pilings with the spade.

They argue over the merits of each fisherman's rock, the number and proportions of the fish they've caught there and the rig they favour for each species. Resting, they become twitchy at the thought of fish. 'Comeon, grabalantern!' They have to talk Phillip out of it, Phillip with his fail-safe method for tarakihi. Frank has long since vacated the rose garden, but they're still wary of opening a window, and opt to squint in the cigarette smoke instead. When they start to feel the constriction of the four walls, nowhere to go, no car to fill with booze and drive away, or women to chase, just clouds and cows, Phillip lights on the idea of raiding the hospital block for pills. It's almost midnight when they physically restrain him from going. He tries to wrench his arms free but his strength is imagined. Patients along the hall stare at their ceilings and weigh up their options. To Jim, the hour has taken on a gravitas. His memory is surging.

He begins talking about his wife to anyone who'll listen. Even fewer than listen to him pity him. They suspect he has squandered a good thing. 'She used to like a drink herself,' he says.

'What a bitch,' Gerald says, and again, 'what a bitch,' but he also has a stake in an arm wrestle. He leans away from Jim and his mariner's grip. Jim just can't seem to impress on anyone the scale of the injustice he has suffered. She stopped making the boozy Spanish Cream he liked. She didn't iron his underwear. She seemed happier to see the slipper salesman than him.

> . . . Where would you normally buy slippers for the family, if you don't mind my asking? But don't rely on my word. The scuff-o-meter it's called, or number of wears before repair. I've had a busy morning on your street, Madam . . .

She didn't talk about planting apple trees anymore. He couldn't remember the last jar she'd labelled 'Zoo Fund' or 'Lolly Collection'. Then he could, and the look he got when he spilled the coins onto the TAB counter. Something else came back to him, from when he himself was knocking on doors: a cat with something wrong with its sinuses, sitting in the corner like a fat, asthmatic Egyptian statue. The owner must have been eighty if she was a day, and right in the sweet spot: hard of hearing, not too poor, but impressed by the words 'numismatics' and 'philately'. She had leaned on her walking frame and passed him pile after pile of her husband's collecting albums, which didn't mean much to her, she'd told him. She'd rather buy things for her grandchildren.

> Was he an expert himself? I understand. That does answer a question I have. They printed hundreds of thousands of these coronation commemoratives, you see. King George too. And the odd bit of damage here and there does reduce

the value, unfortunately. Would it be easier if I took them off your hands for one even sum and that be the end of it? Good. Wise decision, Mrs Bertram. Now, I'm sorry to have to ask you this but it's a travelling profession I'm in . . .

There'd been a jewellery tray on top of her dresser plain as day, but it couldn't be anything so obvious. He found a set of silver napkin rings instead, in a drawer in the china cabinet. A younger version of Mrs Bertram stared out at Jim from her wedding photograph in her high-necked frills, no smiles or skin showing in those days.

'It was the way she looked at me,' he told them. 'She nagged. Told a man what to do in his own house. Top of the charts was the time she said I wasn't in any state to drive them anywhere. I could do them all a favour and crash the car myself, but they weren't getting in.'

Still, the men aren't moved. It's the possibility that he did it to her, that she was better off before she met him, that he can't abide, that prompts him to take exception to Don looking at the body-building magazine, to ask him if he's a nancy, to lunge towards the pages, knock the full ashtray over and start the fracas that will mark the beginning of the end of the session.

★

'Much better, just lost my guts.' Jim's drinking with some out-of-towners at the vice versa dance. They take trips out to the keg in twos and threes.

'Hup—nice tight soccer jersey, twelve o'clock.' An addendum to the rules of pub cricket: four runs for brushing up against a girl's bum (as witnessed by the other players); six for a breast.

'I'll take this one,' Jim says. He knows her.

'Batter up!'

'Off you go, sweetie.' He sets his grass skirt swaying, past the tea ladies in their neckties and the swarthy nurses behind the raffle table, past the doors to outside where the children are chasing each other—it hasn't quite gone eight.

Deidre Murphy's buttocks are shifting under her footie shorts. She's in striped socks, carrying a pair of boots, spikes and all. He'd never have guessed that one of these uniforms had so much potential. 'Aren't you supposed to be wearing those?' he asks.

'They made me take them off. Spikes on the polished floor.'

'What's this?' Quick as a wink he gestures vaguely towards the club badge on her chest. What he encounters is a padded intermediary, not flesh. 'Oops, sorry.'

He's seen her at dances before. When they're together, lined up, she and her friends form a wall of skirts and lips and hips and curled hair. They're happy to refuse a fellow a dance, to send him back defeated, even if Deidre does usually smile at him, and boy does he like a show of teeth.

She's not smiling now. She's looking over his shoulder. He turns around to see. The boys are all holding their arms over their heads to signal the six, straining their seams. One is wearing a hat with fake flowers sewn on. He has to stop himself from laughing.

★

On the short walk from the main block to the office, Jim feels the unmistakeable drift of alcohol in his system. Time stretches out, and for several seconds he can take it all lightly, nothing settles, but when the sun comes out an ancient weariness sinks in. He knocks on the office door and enters to Mrs Mac's greeting. 'What can I do for you?'

'I need the key for the tool shed, please, to get a wheelbarrow.'

'Key for the tool shed. Actually, it should be open. Frank's down there.'

'Right you are.'

'Are you well, Jim?' She speaks from behind spectacles, beneath neatly set hair, between piles of paperwork.

'Fine.' He leans on his trembling hand. Glances back somewhere in the area of her neck.

'Where are you working today?' she asks. He wants to gag from the shaving cream he dabbed into his hair and around his collar.

'Cable Bay, getting shells for your front garden, and seaweed.'

'Do you need Toby?'

'They've got him for the firewood. A barrow will do.' He bows his head in unconscious supplication as he closes the door.

Nothing but varying density of darkness in the gardening shed, then his eyes adjust and it all comes to him: shovels and spiderwebs, light through the cracks, coiled hose in the corner, tomahawk, axe. He can't see what Frank is doing under the bench. 'How goes it Frank?' he says. He doesn't stop, but aims instead for the barrows upended against one wall. He's suffering. His eyes, his pores, his stomach. He'd like to lie down, just there, on the planks, cease all effort. Frank wouldn't mind. But Jim has another cure in mind. 'What are you up to?' He takes the handles of a barrow in his hands.

'Looking out old pots for seedlings,' Frank says. He pulls himself out and straightens up, surprised to be asked. But Jim pushes the barrow out into the ever-changing weather, back onto the road, past the old lock-up and the schoolhouse. He watches the gravel disappearing under the front wheel—leaping forward, leaping forward again—to distract himself. On the climb out of Home Bay he scares a flock of sparrows in the shrubs beside the track and their dull colours swerve away. When he reaches the elevation he stops and looks out, and the breeze lifts the heat off his skin for a moment. He lets the islands, alternating in two and three dimensions, clear his mind.

No one goes to Mai Mai for shells. They won't look for him there. He takes the barrow's weight on the way down with the westerly washing through the pohutukawas. Ice plant grows to where the tide cuts in. Before he sits down he removes what he's carrying in the waistband of his trousers and stands it up between the waxy spikes. Shells are scarce on the beach. There are more pebbles, and the commotion of a miniature wave every few moments. At the far end, which isn't far, is a tiny inlet. It looks as though a creek comes out there, but there's no creek, no water source. A nobody-cares beach on a nobody-cares island. He may as well be a sandhopper.

Last night he took a candle with him to the bathroom to relieve himself and stuck it into the stand beside the mirror. He had some kind of premonition. Owing to a trick of the light or of his mind he saw himself as if he were at least ten years older. He could have been in his fifties, the way his skin sagged under his eyes. Deep furrows ran down from both ends of his mouth to his chin. They resembled something. He couldn't think what, then he could: one of those ventriloquist's dummies, and not a new one. By the look of the eyes, fixed and faded, he'd been touring the circuit for years. He'd dismissed it at the time, shaken his head and gone back for more of what he could get, but in the morning, after he'd shaved and used the flannel, the lines were still there, more prominent than he'd ever noticed them being before.

With his thumb and index finger he traces the gouges from the corners of his mouth now. He picks up the old vinegar bottle he swiped from the kitchen, takes the cork out, lifts it to his lips and tips some of the leftover wine into his mouth. It's warm and acidic. He suppresses his gag reflex for as long as he can, three swallows, then lowers the bottle and breathes. He leans forward and picks up the few rock oyster and pipi shells he's been staring at and tosses them into the wheelbarrow with a tin rattle.

When he was a boy the wheelbarrow was beech, home-made, and it was acorns he'd collected. He'd hoarded vast piles, or they'd seemed vast. He thought of them as a kind of currency. What wealth he enjoyed in his own kingdom. He liked the perfect ones, with unflawed husks, but he also appreciated the flesh inside. If he could get his fingernail into a crack, he could peel the husk off to expose the softer, mottled nut beneath, or split it in two, each half so smooth under his thumb and such a mild colour. He got so much pleasure from collecting them, but they weren't good for anything. He takes another few gulps and finds that he's leaking tears.

He drinks again, and picks up more shells, hears the clatter as they go in. Each time he bends over, pain blooms above his right temple. After a while it shifts somewhere else, then that spot, too, mists over. The water was there long before him and will be there after. It keeps coming, unrelenting. He's given it a shot, but it hasn't worked out, no shame in that. He begins raking stones into his pockets instead. They're good and heavy when the tiny human appears on the shore. He can't quite believe it's real at first: blond head, thick limbs, a seeming indifference to Jim, though a nervous transect of the beach in Jim's direction brings him closer and gives him away, until he is near enough to pick up and throw fistfuls of shells, sand and stones into the barrow indiscriminately, helping. Jim stays silent for a while, lest he frighten him.

Lorna

'Lunchtime, Mrs Vardy.' The nurse's seniority had something to do with how much busier she was: busier than Lorna and her dad, who were sitting and standing beside the bed, and far busier than Lorna's mum, who was lying in it. Visitors were bottom rung. She didn't even use their names. 'You'll have to go now,' she said, and they had to leave Lorna's mum there with her *War Cry* and her *Woman's Weekly* (people who'd been struck down by the worst disasters got a private room). Back out in the starkly lit warren of unfortunates, doctors came and went and wondered, with the door to the dispensary open, whether they were going to fit in a round of golf.

Nerves in her spine had been damaged during surgery and it was going to be worse, not better. They hadn't planned for worse, and for now she was completely reliant on other people.

Talk of a wheelchair and alterations to the house had only brought on a kind of stunned obedience, not that she had any choice but to sit and listen.

She'd alarmed Lorna when they were alone together. 'We shouldn't have forced the adoption on you,' she'd said. 'I can't help but think that this is God's way of telling me we got it wrong.'

'Sometimes things just happen,' Lorna had told her. 'If someone else had adopted him, I wouldn't know where he was.'

When he found his Mama helpless in a bed at the end of corridors buzzing with uniforms, white instead of the black he was used to, Isaac crawled onto Lorna's knee and stayed there for longer than she'd ever known him to. He watched while the patient rubbed her legs, perhaps willing herself to feel some sensation, however faint, and eventually reached his own hand out to stroke the leg nearest him. She grabbed and clasped it fiercely.

'Here love,' she said. 'Hold my hand instead.' Lorna told herself and anyone else who asked that her mum was going to come right, but they didn't know.

Telephone calls. Lorna's dad telephoned Nancy Eng. She told him she would pray and freeze meals for them. Paul phoned Uncle Reg from the island to ask him to take in a change of clothes for her dad, which he did, along with grapes and baking from the Birkenhead Corps, and Nancy Eng herself, pushing her baby in a pram. The nurse was outnumbered by black uniforms the next time she bustled in, and stopped short of ordering them to leave. Lorna and her dad went out anyway, to give Isaac some fresh air. They spent a few minutes in the drizzle tugging him away from the decorative flower beds in Cornwall Park before taking shelter in the hospital's canteen, where they slid sandwiches and sausage rolls on a tray along the rails past the lamingtons they wouldn't let Isaac have, no matter how many times he pointed through the forest of adult limbs. The woman at the till put two wine gums on their tray. 'There you are, luvvie.'

After they sat down, though, a different woman at the next table frowned when Isaac declared out loud how much he was enjoying his lollies. She turned towards them just far enough to show her displeasure (her mouth held set in a line, her large cheek, her pearl knot earring), but not far enough for confrontation. Her husband might have only weeks to live, Lorna reminded herself. No one went to a hospital canteen out of choice.

'Shall I phone Claire and ask if I can take Isaac back with me?' she asked.

'I think it's best for now,' her dad said. 'Doug and Moira are coming down tomorrow.'

None of them had seen Lorna's gran and grandpa since her mum had tried to join them up in the Church of Jesus Christ.

'Do they know about Isaac?' Lorna asked. Isaac pressed his fingers onto the plate and watched the pastry stick to them—gravely, because they were talking about him.

'No, but they've never agreed with our decisions in the past, so I can't see them backing this one.' He hadn't been so blunt with her since he used to have his bad spells, when he'd forget that she was too young to understand. He'd been using a cheerful tone, to convince Isaac that everything was fine, but it gained an edge when he addressed the woman beside them, who was watching Isaac openly now. 'Is everything all right?'

The woman moved her mouth and made an unusual sound, a vague imitation of talking, unusual enough that Isaac began watching her back. She shook her head, pointed to her ears and opened a notepad sitting on the table in front of her. She held it up.

It said, *Sorry, deaf.*

She was smiling back and forth at them now. She peeled back the top leaf and held the pad up again. *My sister is sick.* Lorna's dad reached out for the pad and pencil.

'She can't hear or talk very well,' Lorna told Isaac, 'so we're writing things down instead.' She tried to wipe the pastry crumbs off his fingers with her serviette, holding his wrist so he couldn't pull his hand away, but the flakes stuck to his skin. He would want to pretend that he couldn't hear soon. He would want his own pad and pencil. Her dad tapped the page he'd written on and held the pad out for the woman to take. The woman looked at the pad and beamed her approval around at all of them again, lingering longer than most people would, to be sure they returned it. Without warning, she reached a hand out towards Isaac, perhaps meaning to pat him on the head, but he took fright and shrank away from her. 'She's not going to hurt you,' Lorna said, but he wouldn't budge, and the woman's scolded arm drifted back.

'Better go,' Lorna's dad said. The woman leafed back to the front page of her pad again and held it up.

Sorry, deaf. She used her spurned hand to wave at Isaac.

'Wave goodbye to the lady, Isaac,' Lorna's dad said. Isaac didn't move, he just stared.

Lorna couldn't remember it very well, the time her mum found her crouched on the floor in her gumboots at the

Takapuna house trying to pick shards of broken glass out of the carpet. She had handled the biggest pieces first, oh so carefully, and dropped them in a bucket she'd found. The smaller, glinting slivers had posed more of a problem. They were easier to see if the sun caught them and would stick to her fingers when she pressed the windowsill, but none of that worked when they were embedded in loops of the carpet's pile. As far as she'd been able to tell, her dad was getting stuck in to a job on the house. Breaking the windows happened to be the first step. 'Keep back!' he'd said, and she'd settled in behind him on the lawn, audience to a demolition. To reach the higher windows in the toilet and washroom he'd fetched the stepladder. When they'd shattered, they hadn't made the tinkling sound she'd imagined. The sound was a kind of blat, and he'd had to hit a couple of them more than once with the shovel before the punched-in spiderwebs came tumbling out of the frame. None of that was so strange. She had been surprised that he hadn't laid anything down over the carpet first, no newspaper or tarpaulin. Also, his eyes, which weren't seeing her properly when he looked at her, she could tell.

When her mum got home he was drinking a bottle of beer in the back section, with his feet resting on the upside-down washing basket. 'I wanted to let some fresh air through,' he'd said. Lorna had seen Isaac look similar, in the wheelbarrow with his feet sticking out: safe in one sense, but still lost in another.

Her dad had chosen the side of the house that faced away from the street; that was a small mercy, but there would have been much less mess if he'd stood inside and knocked the windows outwards, Lorna's mum had said. Either way, he got sent off to a 'Sanitarium for reserved servicemen', like the breakfast cereal. Even after Lorna learned it was a sanatorium, she still pictured men like her dad sitting around munching themselves better on Weetbix, because that was the cure: square meals and fresh air. He'd been on the right track to seek fresh air, but he'd gone about it the wrong way. Without him there to sweep the front path, dried bits of stalks and leaves and sand would settle there, whatever was blown over by the wind or carried in.

Lorna made the next telephone call. While she waited for Claire to pick up she wondered if they had the same rain on the island as there was in Greenlane, or a clear patch of sky, or both, off and on. She could picture the phone ringing in the office, a series of long, single rings. When Claire answered, the connection wasn't all that clear, but her voice was enough to bring it all back, the realm of the island, the beauty and the mission. Claire asked after her mum and told her they'd all been praying. Of course Lorna should bring Isaac back with her, she said. It was too quiet without him. She asked after the patients who had travelled back on the *Mahoe* with Lorna, the ones involved in the drinking session. They had kept themselves to themselves near the bow, fidgeting, Lorna told her. 'George went his own way. He told me he'd see me soon.'

'I wouldn't be surprised if he went straight into the Criterion. He told me to keep his room for him.' Claire's voice was cut off for a few moments. '——put your head around the door.'

'Sorry, I didn't hear that.'

'Katherine Morton is there. She had a small stroke last week, if you want to pop in.'

Lorna objected to the constant pressure, the suggestion that she could always be doing more. She might be in God's service, but it was Claire who issued the orders.

'Is she up to seeing visitors?' she asked.

She left Isaac behind when she set out, so he wasn't there to ask in his high voice what the orderlies were doing with the linen, what was wrong with the person on the gurney and where the beeping came from when the lift door opened, but still she lost track of turns and block numbers after a while and had to follow the yellow tape back to the main entrance to ask for Miss Morton's ward. Beyond every door were more patients in need of prayers, but it wouldn't be right to throw them all in together: 'Bless all of the patients at Greenlane' would be too easy. Lorna listened to her footsteps clack neatly on the floor. How much easier it must be to work on the mainland, with so many trained members of staff and modern facilities, everything just outside the doors. The patients at Greenlane hadn't been turned out by society the way theirs had. Theirs were only at home on their way to the bottom of a glass. Even there they made a nuisance of themselves eventually.

When she finally found the right corridor and counted her way along to the appropriate number, the ward sister was disposing of something in a metal bin at the door. 'Are you Lieutenant Hendry?' the sister asked.

Lorna didn't think she was imagining the heightened level of curiosity. 'I'm not family or a close friend,' she said. 'I'm just delivering a message.'

The nurse seemed to relax. 'You're lucky to catch her.' The words came in a rush, faster than before. 'It was a minor event. There was talk of moving her to a private hospital, but she's already improved since yesterday. Go ahead and join them. She's got another visitor.' Lorna half hoped Miss Morton would be asleep so she could leave the card behind and get back.

The ward was brighter than her mum's and lacked a sense of catastrophe. The patients Lorna passed were knitting, chatting and reading. One had a crocheted rug brought from home. Two large windows showed clouds outside and the corner of a building opposite. The curtain was pulled around Miss Morton's bed, so Lorna couldn't see her until she reached the far end of the ward and walked around it.

The journalist's face hadn't dropped, not that Lorna could see. She was wearing make-up and a scarf over her hair, and was surrounded by flowers: lilies, roses, gypsophila. If someone had taken her photograph, it wouldn't have looked out of place in a magazine. Her visitor was pouring a glass of water from a jug that only just fit on the bedside table.

'Hello Lieutenant Hendry,' Miss Morton said. 'It's very kind of you to come.' She spoke more slowly than before, but it might have been tiredness. Her hands were gently clasped in her lap.

'How are you feeling?' Lorna asked.

Miss Morton paused, took a deep breath and ignored Lorna's question. 'This is quite a coincidence, because Colleen's husband is on Rotoroa, or he was.' But Lorna could only take in one coincidence at a time. Colleen was Colleen, from the Sunshine Home. Same pointy chin and nose, same alertness. She didn't look any older. More fashionable, if anything, in her town dress.

'Look at you!' Colleen said. 'You're a Sallie. Come and give me a hug.' It was the same generous hug as when Lorna was the one in the hospital bed. 'We met in Te Atatu a few years back,' Colleen told Miss Morton.

'You obviously got along well,' Miss Morton said.

'We did,' Colleen said. 'Oh my goodness.'

Lorna's heart was thumping. Colleen seemed far more relaxed. 'Look at you, you got even more religious.'

Miss Morton must be wondering how they knew each other. Lorna was wondering the same thing about the two of them.

'Yes, God called me,' she said.

'I didn't know God used the phone,' said Colleen.

In the midst of all the mental commotion, Lorna remembered what she was there for. 'Sorry Miss Morton. I haven't even given you this—from all of us.' She held the card out to her. 'How are you feeling?'

'I'll live. That's very nice,' Miss Morton said. 'Put it up here, beside the vase. I'm glad you didn't bring flowers. I feel as though I'm in my own—' her brow creased. 'Box.' A pause. 'Coffin.'

Colleen met Lorna's eye. 'You've been keeping an eye on my no-hoper husband over on the island,' she said.

'Who's your husband?'

'Jim Brooks.'

'Jim Brooks? But—'

'I know, I know. He's messed it up. The police are trying to decide what to do with him.' She had the same way of shrugging things off as ever, but now she took hold of one of her elbows with the other hand as if cradling herself.

'We both came out on the same boat yesterday,' Lorna said. 'I've seen quite a bit of him.'

'When I missed morning tea,' Miss Morton said, 'it was

Jim I spoke to. Do you remember?'

Colleen shook her head. 'He gets around, doesn't he?' She didn't quite achieve the light-heartedness she was reaching for.

'He came to our evening service last night,' Lorna said. 'He doesn't usually.'

'Must have known he was in trouble,' Colleen said.

'Still, that might be a good sign,' Miss Morton said. 'Perhaps we ought to say a prayer. Do you think? Would you mind, Lorna?'

'Of course not,' Lorna said, though having Colleen there made her feel whitewashed. Everybody has their own spiritual gifts, she'd been told at college. Everyone can serve in their own way. Lorna might not have the same faith as some, but if she could help, did it matter? She bowed her head with them.

'Dear Lord,' she said. 'We thank you for your blessings, including the blessing of being together. Please bless especially Katherine Morton, Jim Brooks and my mother Rae. Watch over those we have lost, Lord. Amen.'

'Amen,' Colleen mumbled.

'Amen,' Miss Morton said. 'Thank you.' Her smile faded, as though the prayer had taken the last of her energy. She hadn't shifted her position or gestured in the time Lorna had been there. At that moment, her scarf and make-up seemed out of place, a forced or failed attempt. She didn't resemble a person who had traversed glaciers and driven around the Middle East in a jeep. 'What did you say you were doing in town?' she asked.

Lorna waited for a patient on the other side of the curtain to finish a bout of coughing. 'I'm here with family. My mother had an operation on her spine.' It was the first time she'd thought about her mum since she'd entered the ward.

'And is she recovering well?' Miss Morton asked.

'The operation didn't go very well,' Lorna said. 'It went badly, actually. She doesn't have sensation in her legs at the moment.' She wished she did have the gift of faith, then.

'God,' Colleen said, then quickly apologised. 'I shouldn't have said that.'

'And here I was soaking up all the sympathy,' Miss Morton said.

'Not at all,' Lorna said.

'So you came because it's your duty, no matter what your personal circumstances.' In the way she turned her bedsheet over the blanket and smoothed it down, her right hand a little ungainly, Miss Morton somehow showed her approval. 'And what about your brother?' she asked. 'You were going to collect him the last time I saw you.'

Careful, Lorna thought.

'Have you always had a brother?' Colleen asked.

'He's just little,' Lorna said. 'He's four in May.' Colleen looked at her frankly, then at Miss Morton's blanket.

'He's been staying with us on the island,' Lorna said. Jim had brought him back, Colleen's Jim. She thought of Isaac on the track, with a drop on one side of him and the sky behind, almost as if he were dangling in space. Losing him had put a fear into her she didn't think she'd ever be able to shake.

Colleen was still examining the lump of Miss Morton's knees. 'He's not here in the hospital is he?'

'Who?' Lorna asked.

'Your brother.'

'Oh, I could do with seeing a four-year-old,' Miss Morton said. 'They're the best cure I know for low spirits.'

'Just as well they can cure them, because mine can cause

240

them too.' This time Colleen fell short of dissatisfaction. Her love was too obvious.

'And your husband, is he here?' Miss Morton asked Lorna.

'Your husband? Who are you married to?'

'His name's Paul,' Lorna said. 'He's on the island, working.'

'The dark glasses he wears, is that an ailment?' Miss Morton said.

'He injured his eyes when he was younger,' Lorna said. 'He used to wear them all the time, but he's improving.'

'My son Derek wants glasses,' Colleen said. 'He decided he likes them for some reason.'

'Isaac's the same,' Lorna said. 'He wants what everyone else has got.'

'Heaven forbid,' Miss Morton said.

'They won't like it when it happens,' Colleen said. 'They just want a fuss made of them.'

That might have been what her dad had wanted, Lorna thought, back when she was still young: for someone to make a fuss, instead of carrying on as though nothing had happened.

'Go and get him Lorna,' Colleen said. 'How much longer are visiting hours ?'

'Four, I think. Ask the sister,' Miss Morton said.

The patient on the other side of the curtain was coughing again, labouring away at it. Lorna could see her now, partially reflected in a set of stainless steel cabinet doors. Her tipped-forwards head, and her slumped shape in her gown. Someone should pour her a glass of water, Lorna thought, or rub her back, but the knitting needles were still clicking and sliding on the other side of the room where the nearest patient and her visitors formed a huddle. Their chatter had even raised a notch or two in volume to overcome the interruption.

Lorna turned back to the two women. 'I'll see if I can bring him back, then,' she said. Isaac wasn't going to escape his fate. All the way across the blocks and up and down hallways, just to find two strange ladies at the end who wanted to pat his head. She left them more animated than she had found them. On the other side of the curtain, the ward sister had arrived beside the bed of the coughing patient and was pouring out a measure of something. Lorna didn't feel like waiting for her to finish, so she carried on and stepped out into the corridor.

'Excuse me,' she said. The orderly was in white short-sleeves and almost camouflaged by the walls, an accessory of the hospital. It wasn't until she reached him that she realised he was near her age, and good-looking. He might be a university student. Whatever he was, he was more difficult to speak to than the ward sister or knitting woman would have been. 'Is it four o'clock visiting finishes?' she asked.

His trolley was covered by a sheet. The object underneath was square, not a person, thank goodness.

'That's a bit above my training,' he said. There wasn't any one thing about him. It was a combination of features—perhaps colour in his cheeks, perhaps his vivid eyes—that clicked home.

'Oh, I'm sorry.'

'Just pulling your leg. It's four.' A joke. It asked more of her than simple gratitude, but she didn't know what, which was probably just as well.

'Thank you,' she said.

'Not a bother.' Neither of them moved for a moment. It was only a beat, then he pushed his trolley out in front of himself and caught it, and Lorna continued down the corridor. She felt charged up. The light from overhead wasn't stark now, but bathed everything in a smooth sheen. At first she heard only the rattle of the trolley's wheels behind her, then she heard humming. He was humming to himself, or—perhaps—to her. Click, click, click, went her footsteps. She was conscious of the movement of her hips. Just for a moment, in the clean corridor, she felt a momentum gathering.

Her legs could carry her all the way to the front entrance and out. There was nothing to stop her, no security guards or police officers, no one brandishing a holy book. She could buy a ticket to America, for example, sit on a plane and go there. Why not? For once she not only knew it was possible in the physical sense; she actually believed she could do it.

The orderly's humming faded. When Lorna turned her head, tentatively at first then all the way, he'd gone, had rounded a corner or pushed his trolley through a door. Click, click, click. Her footfalls were hollow again, ordinary, and the charge left her. The paint on the walls was smooth because it had been thickly applied. If anything, it was crude. She remembered something she'd heard them say on the island. It was all very well having flashes of inspiration, they'd say. The thing was, you had to keep having them. She rounded a corner of her own and pointed herself at the lifts. She was going to collect Isaac, then come back. She thought she could remember the way.

Author's note

This book was inspired and furnished by material I found at the Salvation Army Heritage Centre & Archives, the Alcoholics Anonymous Archives and, online, at Ngā Taonga Sound & Vision and Papers Past.

Among the books I read, I often referred to *Set Free: One Hundred Years of Salvation Army Addiction Treatment in New Zealand 1907–2006* (Flag Publications, 2013) by Don and Joan Hutson, and *Real Modern: Everyday New Zealand in the 1950s and 1960s* (Te Papa Press, 2015) by Bronwyn Labrum.

The books of Katherine Morton's I drew the most from were *The Crusoes of Sunday Island* (G. Bell and Sons, 1957), *A Message from England* (Unity Press, 1942) and *Sunrise at Midnight* (Oswald-Sealy and Unity Press, 1948).

Most of the time the portrayals of Katherine Morton and Robert and Claire McCallum stay close to the details of their backgrounds, but the scenes depicted in the novel are invented. Frank is based more loosely on a patient who spent time on the island. Dates have been shifted or conflated occasionally: for example, the term 'patient' instead of 'inmate' was not introduced until slightly later, in the 1960s.

A number of people helped me to find information or were generous in sharing their knowledge and experience, or both. Thanks in particular to Sue Wilkins and Geoff Boyd for getting me started, Paul and Susan Jarvis and Ross Wardle at the Salvation Army Heritage Centre and Archive, Chris at the Alcoholics Anonymous Archives, Ginnene and Phil Salisbury on the island, Karyn Clare at the Rotoroa Island Trust, and for recollections Christie and Angus, Garry Mellsop, Don Hutson, Ruth Grey, Walnetta McCall and Gloria Manson.

I'd like to acknowledge the support and advice Anna Rogers gave me while I was writing and thank Rose Collins, who read a late draft.

Thanks to everyone at Victoria University Press, especially to publisher Fergus Barrowman, editor Ashleigh Young and Kirsten McDougall for sending the book on its way.

My friends and family have been gathered into this effort too. Thanks and love to them, and to Steve for conversations about treatment and fishing, and for everything else.